BIKES ROCKETS

INTERSECTIONAL FEMINIST BICYCLE SCIENCE FICTION STORIES

EDITED BY

ELLY BLUE

MICROCOSM PUBLISHING

PORTLAND, OR

BIKES NOT ROCKETS
INTERSECTIONAL FEMINIST BICYCLE SCIENCE FICTION STORIES

Edited by Elly Blue
All content © its creators, 2018
Final editorial content © Elly Blue, 2018
This edition © Elly Blue Publishing, an imprint of Microcosm Publishing, 2018
First printing, December 10, 2018
All work remains the property of the original creators.

ISBN 978-1-62106-543-2

Elly Blue Publishing, an imprint of Microcosm Publishing
2752 N Williams Ave.
Portland, OR 97227

Cover art by Cecila Granata
Back cover art by Elly Bangs
Inside cover art by Paul Abbamondi
Design by Joe Biel
Special thanks to Cynthia Marts for editorial support

Elly Blue Publishing, an imprint of Microcosm Publishing
2752 N Williams Ave
Portland, OR 97227

This is Bikes in Space Volume 5
For more volumes visit BikesInSpace.com
For more feminist bicycle books and zines visit TakingTheLane.com

If you bought this on Amazon, I'm so sorry because you could have gotten it cheaper and supported a small, independent publisher at MicrocosmPublishing.com

To join the ranks of high-class stores that feature Microcosm titles, talk to your local rep: In the U.S. **Como** (Atlantic), **Fujii** (Midwest), **Travelers West** (Pacific), **Brunswick** in Canada, **Turnaround** in Europe, **New South** in Australia and New Zealand, and **Baker & Taylor Publisher Services** in Asia, India, and South Africa.

Library of Congress Cataloging in Publication Control Number: 2018028333

[TABLE OF CONTENTS]

INTRODUCTION

During the 2008 elections, I was on a rocket to the stars. Hope had always been my thing—hope for a better world, for the exciting possibilities of the bicycle movement, for the next year always being better than the one before. I was ecstatically hopeful about the candidate from Illinois. The night he was elected, I pedaled past the local Democratic campaign headquarters, precariously hands-free, high-fiving the cheering passengers in the cars to my left and the crowd overflowing off the sidewalk to my right.

The following eight years did a number on my hope, though. The economic crash that had been coming on for years finally caught up with me. I entered my thirties and had some mellowing out and growing up to do. The manic energy that had fueled a career based on a vision of bicycling as the perfect solution for all the world's woes slowly fizzled out, especially as I began to wake up to racism—my own, the bike movement's, this country's, and the world's. This awareness came via the news and talk and realizations, coming mostly over Twitter. Obama's election had paved the way for a great, national reckoning with race, and those of us who'd previously had the privilege of cluelessness could no longer imagine an upward-sloping line of progress when it came to racism.

During those early years, I was building my platform on making the bicycle movement aware of sexism. But becoming slowly aware of the movement's racism was, unexpectedly, the key to a personal as well as a political transformation. Instead of seeing myself as a glowing protagonist, I had to come to grips with the reality that my story was not always the neutral one, that I was not always on the side of the underdog, that the certainties I held, even about such seemingly-neutral topics as the paint and pavement of bicycle infrastructure, didn't always represent positive progress for everyone and could even do harm. Shortly after the election, I joined my life and career with a tall white man whose experience of marginality I had trouble accepting even after his diagnosis with autism a few years later, even as I was given credit for his achievements and welcomed into places where he was dismissed. The tools I had learned to think about race were the same ones I needed to see the broken places in my relationship and in my work. I learned to see that my feminism and bicycle activism had to be intersectional, that neither one could stand alone as a single metric or issue. This is what got me off the cloud of hope that had been barely sustaining me for so many years, and brought me down, not into the pit of hopelessness, but to the ground of purpose. And when the election of 2016 came along, it wasn't so much a shock and surprise as it was a call to action.

One of the things I realized in that time was just how much of bicycle advocacy was being conducted by and on behalf of the needs of white, professional, cis men—even though most people actually out there riding didn't seem to fit that description. What's the point? I thought hopelessly. Then I started to see just how much advocacy and movement-building was being done by and for others, that I simply hadn't been able to see. Once I started to look, it was everywhere. My partner and I made a series of short movies showcasing different people and groups we met, running out of funding long before we ran out of stories. The bicycle movement is a microcosm of society, and science fiction is the same, if not worse, in these regards. Many, if not most, readers and writers are not white guys, but that can be hard to see if you aren't looking for it, despite a growing movement and the mainstream successes of a few deserving authors.

The Bikes in Space series of anthologies, of which this is the fifth volume, has grown along with me. I always intended it to be inclusive and intersectional, but at the beginning I assumed that my good intentions, my identification with the underdog, and my glorious vision were enough. They weren't. Like bicycling and feminism, science fiction doesn't exist in a vacuum, and to pretend it does and ignore what is happening in the present—and how it shapes our imagination of the future—is essentially to give in to hopelessness, and probably to white supremacy too.

So with every volume I try to do it a little better. The call for submissions for this volume was for stories on the theme of "Intersections." Intersectionality really has to be the theme of every volume, or what's the point? But in this case, specifically stating it turned out to be an effective way to attract a larger than normal number of excellent stories by talented writers. I've tried to follow the guidance of Nalo Hopkinson (whose excellent novel *Brown Girl in the Ring* features an escape by bicycle through a devastated future Toronto) in her blog post for anthology editors on how to create diverse anthologies without tokenizing authors, or other such jerk moves.

What's the purpose of obsessing about this intersectional approach? Partly it's to help, in a small way, to transform the genre and open up access to the tough supply economy that writing and publishing have become. But most of all, because it makes for better stories. So that more readers can see themselves reflected in someone's vision of the future. So we can deepen our ideas and arguments about what kind of future we can have, and whether or not there's any hope, or any point.

The stories in this volume, however, all do suggest a point. They show people reaching out to each other and working together, despite the odds and across great barriers—personal differences, class, nation, gender, species, and even time. Like all good science fiction should, they speculate about the limits of our humanity, our flexibility, our potential, and the choices we allow ourselves and each other. There's hope to be found in that—our potential to help each other forward.

I do hope you enjoy these stories and that they inspire you to dream up bigger and better ones of your own.

- Elly Blue, Portland, Oregon

LEAVING

Monique Cuillerier

Are you ready to Leave?

Register now for preferred locations!

The sign was on the side of the sagging building where the grocery store used to be. Above the words was a picture of a smiling family gathered at a round window, the clouds of Venus in the background.

Public presentation Thursday, June 12th at 7:30pm.

All your questions answered by Offplanet Immigration specialist.

Simone sighed and continued to ride along what was left of the main road, maneuvering the aging bike around the ever-increasing potholes. The last thing she wanted was a sign berating her. She wasn't the only one, she thought, not for the first time.

The town was smaller these days, different of course, but she felt the same attachment to it that she always had, potholes or no. Living on the water, the crash of the waves as she woke, the sound of the gulls, the tang of salt ever-present in the air, there was nothing on Mars or Titan or anywhere else that would compare.

She liked where she was. And, really, not everyone would need to leave.

The latest attempt at a complete evacuation of the Canadian east coast had begun six months before. The federal government had depended on individuals making the decision to move either inland or off-planet on their own, but that had been insufficient. Too many had held on and they were being pushed further and further back. The costs to maintain the increasingly threatened communities could no longer be born easily.

Inland migration was still possible, but it had become obvious to most people that off-planet migration was the only reasonable long-term choice.

Glancing at her watch, she thought about the preparations required for the two o'clock tour group. Dan would be around somewhere, he spent most of his time at the shop whether a group was booked or not, but it was her responsibility to prepare for the tours.

"Watch out!"

The warning came from nowhere. Simone jerked her head up while automatically braking. Her back wheel skidded, and she hit the edge of a deep hole with the front one, throwing her off the bike.

"Are you okay? I'm so sorry I startled you."

Simone did not recognize the woman speaking in the passing glance she gave her. Struggling up, she walked back to the bike, brushing dirt and gravel from her pants and stretching experimentally to see if anything was injured.

"I really am sorry," the woman repeated, walking after her, "but the turtle…"

Simone turned. The woman was, perhaps, her age, late twenties, maybe older, maybe younger, hard to tell. Her black hair was worn up and her clothing said professional of some sort.

"Turtle?"

"Are you okay?" the woman asked again, concern radiating from her eyes. Simone stopped and took stock of the situation. The woman had been walking along the road, wearing improbable shoes and carrying a bulging messenger bag. In the middle of the road, slowly making its way between the potholes was a large leatherback turtle.

"I think so," Simone said, chastened. "The turtle…"

"She blends in, doesn't she? I saw her just as you went past me."

"We don't get them very often anymore..."

"I'm sure."

The woman was, Simone thought, so pretty. The opposite of Mallory in almost every way, but striking nonetheless.

"I should introduce myself. I'm Simone."

"Lilith," the woman said, shaking the offered hand. "You live here?"

"All my life. I own the dive shop."

"I haven't gone diving in years," the woman said. "Do you do tours?"

Simone smiled. "Indeed we do, of the old town for the most part."

"That sounds amazing. Do you need recent experience to do that? I used to be certified, but it's been awhile."

"We offer an option that works for just about anyone. More experienced divers go further out, explore on their own. But there is something for everyone," Simone said as she slipped into her promotional role.

"Maybe I should do that while I'm here," Lilith said with a smile back at Simone. Her eyes shone and Simone felt a flutter of interest that she had not felt in a long time.

"How long are you here for? Are you on holiday?" Tourists still came, of course, for the diving, just to see the shore, the ocean.

"A week, maybe a bit longer. I'm here on business, maybe you saw the posters? I work for Offplanet Immigration."

"Oh," Simone managed, the flutter stopping abruptly.

"I know. If you're not someone who has already filled out the paperwork, you probably don't want to talk to me. But this area, you have a low registration rate. I'm here to talk to people, to find out why. Maybe come up with some ideas on how to change that."

"We like it here."

"I'm sure you do."

Despite the woman's job, Simone found herself looking at her curiously. She seemed friendly, definitely attractive. Merely entertaining the thought of another woman's attractiveness felt like a betrayal. It didn't matter how long it had been, she thought it always would.

"I have to go," Simone said abruptly. "I have a tour." And with a brisk nod of her head, she got back on her bike and left without a backward glance.

•   •   •

"On your right," Simone began as the tour boat pulled away from the pier, "you will see signs of the old town."

The boat was full with the usual array of visiting diving enthusiasts. Simone faced them, using a mic as the wind whipped at her hair and her nostrils filled with the salty tang of the ocean. They would do a little tour around the current shore, as Dan referred to it, and then head out to where Simone preferred to conduct the dives.

"You can see the top of the cupola of the Central United Church, which was situated on Cumberland Street, four blocks straight up the hill from the original waterfront."

A familiar twisting feeling came to her as she said the words. Repetition had not lessened their impact.

The boat made its way further out and Simone pointed to the buoys that marked the spots where some of the other submerged buildings lay.

Simone often wondered what had happened, as the warnings had become unignorable, the slow, inescapable creep. The water higher on the wharf, lapping over it. The sense of resignation as the closest buildings went up for sale, one by one, with no buyers in sight and the water coming closer, enveloping, taking back.

She shook her head and returned her attention to the task at hand.

"We will be arriving at the dive site in a few moments. Let's begin with reviewing our procedures," she said.

·   ·   ·

"How long have you two lived here?" Thierry, one of the divers from the afternoon, asked Simone and Dan. He, and another one of the divers, Jen, had invited Simone and Dan to join them for a post-dive drink. They were in the pub closest to the water. A small building, it had been decorated to recreate the old town.

"All my life," Dan answered and Simone nodded in agreement.

"Wow," Thierry said, "you must have seen things change."

"The biggest changes happened a long time ago," Simone began. "The water is still rising, but it is more of a slow, relentless thing now. The old life is long gone, but I don't know what that might have been like. My grandmother used to talk about it, when the tourists still came for the old town. Of course," and she nodded at the two strangers, "we still get tourists. For now."

She had to keep reminding herself that the clock was winding now. It didn't feel like it.

"My great-grandpa was still alive when I was small," Dan added, "and he talked a lot about it. More people came then and there were a lot more local people, of course."

Thierry nodded. His companion Jen asked, "When are you leaving?"

Thierry shot her a look. Simone could tell he thought the question inappropriate. She didn't know how to even begin answering, so she was glad Dan took the lead.

"My family's paperwork is in," Dan said simply. "There's me and my wife and we have two boys. Living here, doing this, is what I always wanted.

When I was a kid, I thought the best possible life would be if I could spend all day on a boat on the ocean." He laughed. "And that's what I've gotten to do for the last ten years! I honestly could not be happier that I got to have that. My kids won't."

Jen looked apologetic.

"It's okay," Dan continued. "The time has come. We put in our request. Hopefully, we'll get what we asked for. We're going to Mars if we have. The opposite of here, isn't it?"

The colonies on Mars and the Moon were now well-established. And those on Titan and Enceladus were, although in their infancy, coming along and increasing in size every year. The cloud-based colony-station orbiting Venus had almost reached capacity and a second was planned. There had been setbacks, of course, but the exodus from Earth had been easier, in many respects, than expected.

Jen turned to Simone, "And where are you going?"

"I don't know," she confessed. She felt the panicked discomfort she got from the posters. "I just… I mean, I live in the house my great-grandfather built and I'm the last of my family. I'd like to see other places, I suppose, but it's never been the most important thing. I guess travel would be nice, but I have never wanted to actually leave."

In a sudden moment of clarity, and without thinking about what she was saying, Simone blurted out, "I am afraid that, if I leave, I will forget."

An uncomfortable silence descended over the table.

"Oh," said Jen finally. "The town?"

Simone sighed. "I don't want to forget all the little details. I want to hold onto them tightly. Everyone can't leave, can they?"

Quietly, Dan said, "That's exactly what they want, though."

Thierry spoke. "This is our farewell tour," he said plainly. Simone knew it was something that people were doing. Lots of people.

"Where are you going? Don't you worry?"

"You mean, about what Venus will be like when we get there? Yes."

Simone thought about that. She could not imagine being anywhere but here. "Where are you from?" she asked.

"Toronto," Jen answered.

"Montreal," said Thierry.

"How do you know each other?" Simone wondered.

"We were grouped by the Leaving centre. When we applied. They say people do better with a support group. They match you for interests. We both liked diving and stuff, so here we are."

Simone didn't know what to make of it all.

"I love the Earth," Jen said abruptly. "I really do, but I can't stay. If those of us who can leave don't, what will happen to the people who can't? We all know the Earth can't support us all anymore. Some of us need to leave. For everyone's sake."

Simone had heard that argument before. And intellectually, she understood it. In reference to herself it was so much more complicated.

"We've taken so much from the Earth," Thierry chimed in, "we need to pull back. What are the alternatives? The planet cannot support the number of people on it now. It is impossible. It's not that I want to necessarily leave, just that I know that some of us have to."

"I've always wanted to go into space," Jen volunteered. "I read all the old SF—Clarke, Heinlein, Burroughs—and that is what I wanted, those possibilities! It's not that I don't love the Earth. Really. It's just... I want to explore."

Simone was quiet. She did not know what to make of their confessions.

"Don't you have family?" she wondered aloud. She didn't know why she asked.

"My parents are dead," Jen said baldly. "I have a brother, we don't talk often. He lives in Banff. We can talk just as easily if I'm orbiting Venus, to be honest. I'm a programmer, I can do that wherever I am."

"That's it, I think," Thierry continued. "Both my parents are still alive, but we see each other once or twice a year. They live in northern Quebec, where I grew up. I don't go up very often and they almost never visit me. If we're going to talk by video link, it doesn't matter where each of us is, does it? I'm actually an engineer. I have a job waiting for me on Venus, way more interesting than anything available here."

Simone listened. It was like watching something on the net. They were so casual about leaving. She had seen the ads—Mars: Will you be chosen? You need to sign up first! and Will you take the first step towards Venus? But to eat and drink with people who were committed, who had a schedule for Leaving—that was something outside of her understanding.

Dan said, "I know people are already there, but so much is unknown."

Thierry nodded excitedly, "Exactly. I can't wait to get there. It's going to be awesome."

Simone looked out the window at the crashing waves. She felt separate from those who were so sure of themselves. The reappearance of the posters, the plans people were making, she could not relate to their interest, their excitement.

Why would she leave this place that had her genetics impressed upon it, her memories—her grandparents, her parents. Mallory.

Mallory. So serious, always biting her bottom lip, eyes downcast as she thought out some solution mysterious to Simone.

Mallory. The softness of her skin and the small noises she made while she thought. The unexpected ferocity with which held on to Simone when they made love.

"Do you mind if I join you?" someone asked. It was the Offplanet Immigration woman.

"Sure," Simone said. "Long day?"

Lilith smiled and put her beer down on the table. Simone turned to the others, "This is Lilith," she said. "She works for Offplanet."

"Are you the one speaking at the meeting tomorrow?" Dan asked.

"I am. Are you Leaving?"

"I am," Dan answered with a smile. "We're going to Mars."

"Mars is a nice place. So is Venus."

"Thierry and I are going to Venus," said Jen

"That's exciting. I lived on Titan for a few years. I came back for this job. It means a lot to me."

"Hmm," was all Simone said and took a deep drink from her beer.

Lilith considered her, drained her beer, and motioned to the server for another. She didn't say anything else until it came.

"I do know where you're coming from, Simone. I grew up in the Marshall Islands."

Simone paused at that. The Marshall Islands had been the first complete loss.

"I'm sorry," she mumbled.

"Obviously I've come to terms with it, but it's all gone. So I do know what you feel. I understand what you're worried about. I know about leaving."

But she doesn't know everything, Simone thought rebelliously, feeling like a teenager.

"My family had lived and died there for… well, who knows how long?"

"But when you left, there was nothing, was there?"

"We lived on one of the atolls that sat a little higher in the water. We weren't the first to be lost. But we had to go. Some stayed while the water rose."

Simone had heard of that happening, not just in the Pacific islands, but elsewhere, too. Sometimes people could not believe the worst, even when it was so clear.

This town, her town, would be gone at some point. The mitigation plans would be exhausted, the seawall insufficient.

"I have to go," Simone said as she stood up and grabbed her jacket. "I hope your time here is successful," she said to Lilith and gave a nod to the others.

She could not describe the feeling inside her as she stalked out into the coolness of the early evening. She wanted Mallory so much.

As she walked, she tried not to think of any of it, but the memories of that last day were as vivid as if they had just happened.

The argument over where to go for dinner. Simone walking out of Mallory's house much like this.

"Whatever," she had called over her shoulder, the last thing she ever said to Mallory. And she had kicked at the bike, her bike now, but Mallory's then, as she walked past. She had gone to the dive shop to cool off, and it had worked. Within a couple of hours she was feeling bad for her behavior, although the feeling—one she did not dwell on now—that perhaps the relationship was not working out was strong in her mind when she picked up her phone to call Mallory and apologize.

But there was no answer, so she left work to head over to the house.

She was barely at the main road when she saw the flashing lights of a police car, a fire truck, and an ambulance with it's back doors open. A crowd stood in the middle of an intersection. She could barely breathe, but she started to run. She was almost at the group when someone caught her and held her and told her not to go closer. It was the police chief and the look he gave her held such pity she knew there was no possibility for anything other than what she feared.

Mallory, angry still Simone was sure, had gone out on her bike—now miraculously unharmed—and been hit by one of the few trucks left in town.

Maybe it was a fluke that it happened when it did. Maybe she had been distracted. It was impossible for Simone to know, but she blamed herself every day.

She never dwelled on their relationship, per se—its lack of staying power, its newness at the time, because that did not seem so important really. Mallory's death mattered.

Simone shook her head and made her way down the short path to her front door. It was still early, but she felt very tired.

•   •   •

"Simone?" She looked up from the counter in the dive shop. Lilith was standing in the doorway. "I was wondering if I could arrange a dive?"

Simone looked at the woman speculatively. She felt a twinge inside.

"What did you want to do?"

"I'd love to get out past the original waterfront."

Simone smiled slightly. "Do you want to go now?"

"Can we?"

"Why not?"

Simone rose. "Dan!" she called out the back door. "I'm taking the small boat."

"Come on," she said to Lilith.

"Will he mind?" Lilith asked as Simone led her to the equipment shed.

"No, he's fine. Anyway, all this is mine," and she spread out her arms to indicate the dive shop, the shed, and the boat house below them on the water. "And there are no scheduled tours this afternoon."

"Is that often the case?" she asked as they went into the shed and Simone began flipping through a rack of wet suits. "That you don't have anyone?"

"It varies. What are you, about 165 cm?"

"Yes. Well, 163," Lilith answered in surprise.

Simone pulled out a suit. "I think this one will fit. I do it every day," she said with a smile.

She grabbed air tanks from beside a table and carried them out. "You'll find the rest of the gear on the wall to your right. I'll be right back."

$\bullet \qquad \bullet \qquad \bullet$

The boat made its way out past the church spire and the clusters of buoys. Simone had taken one of the smaller boats, with no cabin, only a small shade canopy from the sun. She sat at the wheel while Lilith perched on the side, looking curiously around her.

"Are the buoys for buildings close to the surface?"

"You got it. The church spire is the only thing tall enough to still see, but there are—well, you can see how many are close."

"We didn't have any tall buildings, not on the atoll I'm from anyway. There was nothing left when the water rose."

That image hit Simone hard and it suddenly occurred to her that she was quite dependent on what she could see, on knowing that, though the old harbor was gone, the old buildings submerged, she could spend time with them whenever she wanted.

Lilith's long black hair was loose, the wind whipping it about. She turned and smiled at Simone. "This is beautiful. I miss the ocean."

"That's one of the things I don't want to lose," Simone said suddenly from a place of fear and worry.

"Of course, you don't want to lose it. But what can we do? You know what is happening. It is simply too expensive for us to maintain human settlements here."

Simone had heard the rationale and it wasn't that it didn't make sense.

It was more personal than that.

Mallory. The bike. The shop. Her family.

They reached a line of buoys. "This is the old waterfront."

"Amazing," Lilith said and moved to prepare her equipment for the dive. "How deep?"

And with that Simone submerged herself in the professional duties she was accustomed to. They readied themselves and checked each other. And then one after the other, they slid into the water.

Simone felt her earthbound worries vanish in the clarity of the ocean. The shapes below them were easily discerned. Not recognizable, of course, unless you knew what you were headed towards. The buildings here had been mostly made from wood, and they had not been newly built when they were taken by the water. What remained of them was delicate, frozen in this watery grave.

Simone continued down.

It had been very gradual, the water, the movement to higher ground, and the buildings' contents had been emptied almost entirely, but the sunken village that remained was fascinating. There was a peacefulness about it that was in keeping with the caress of the water and that was what Simone most liked.

Slowly, Simone became aware of Lilith motioning to her. She swam over.

Lilith was near the remains of the pier, where the water used to meet the land. Debris was spread out, shifted to and fro by the motion of the tides. At this point the buildings stopped and, beyond, the natural order of the ocean was restored.

As she came up beside the other woman, Simone saw the glinting of something stuck in the sand and Lilith moved to release it. In that moment, as Lilith pulled the object out of the accumulated sand and silt, there was something in her movement, the tilt of her head, that made Simone think it was Mallory.

She worried that, if she left, when she left, these moments caught in time would be forever lost.

•   •   •

"Is it too early for dinner?" Lilith asked as they checked and put away the gear. "I'd like to take you out to eat."

Simone paused and felt herself withdraw. "You can't convince me to sign up."

Lilith was taken aback. "I wasn't going to badger you over dinner."

Silently, Simone finished hanging up the wetsuits.

"Where can we go? Is there anywhere other than the bar?"

Simone internally debated what to do. There were a couple of restaurants—a place with pizza and burgers and another a bit fancier.

"Why don't I make you dinner at my place?" she blurted before she could think too much about it. "I have more than enough for both of us."

"Oh," Lilith said, taken aback. "I wasn't angling for an invite."

"Of course not. Do you like pasta? Any preferences?"

She smiled at Lilith. She really was beautiful, with the flowing black hair and skin that seemed to glow from inside. Her dark eyes looked at Simone steadily and she smiled back.

"Let's go."

.   .   .

"This is lovely," Lilith said. Simone's kitchen was not particularly large, but there was a raised ledge for eating and bar stools along it. She liked to think of it as compact.

"Thank you."

"You've always lived here, but in this house?"

"I grew up here. I went away for university, but I came back when I was done."

"You must really love it."

"I do," Simone said softly.

"Don't you ever think about going elsewhere?"

Simone continued chopping peppers for some time before she spoke. "Not really. Not now."

"What do you mean?"

She took a deep breath, wondering if she was prepared to say anything. "I did, at a time. My girlfriend, she wanted to leave. But it was a long time ago and we weren't together very long."

"Did she leave?"

Simone's breath caught. "Yes…in a way."

"Oh," Lilith said.

"We weren't together that long. But here I am, still here."

"Unsaid, undone things…"

"It was just shocking in the moment, you know? Now, she's a larger presence in my life than she was when she was alive."

"I felt like that about my home for a while. Not that I didn't love it, I did. But I loved it more when it was gone. The missing was stronger."

"But you left…"

"Earth, you mean? Yes. The atoll was gone. I could have lived elsewhere, nearby I suppose. I had a girlfriend who took me in a different direction. She wanted to go and so go we went. Titan wasn't her first choice, but it was where they sent us and I loved it. So different than anything Marshallese, but it was like I was made for it."

"And then you came back?"

"Temporarily, yes. This job takes me all over. I've been to the Venusian colony and the Moon. It's Mars after this and then back home to Titan. I like the new places—I love them, really. But the travel—well, it takes time. And in that time, I draw and I write and then I'm in a new place."

"And your girlfriend?"

Lilith gave a small laugh. "For all her begging me to go, she hated it. Completely. Didn't suit her in the least. She came back to Earth several years ago."

"Have you seen her on this trip?" Simone wanted to take back the words as soon as they were out of her mouth.

"We don't see each other anymore. It didn't… end well. She wanted me to come back with her, couldn't understand I actually liked Titan. She thought I should choose her over the place. Maybe I should have. Maybe I would have in a different situation."

"We never know what a choice will truly be until we've chosen."

"No."

Simone turned back to the meal. It was almost done now, the pasta drained, the sauce bubbling, cheese grated into a small bowl in front of her.

"Why don't you sit down at the dining table? It's through there. I'll bring things in."

·　　　·　　　·

She left the bike, Mallory's bike, lying on the sparse sand of the beach and climbed up on the rocks.

Standing there, with the waves crashing just below her feet, Simone looked out towards the horizon.

The dinner last night with Lilith had given her a lot to think about. Mostly, she had felt exhausted and sad, but by morning had felt something different. A realization of sorts that the choice to go was solely in her hands, had always been, and it wasn't right to pretend that her ancestors or the town or even Mallory should hold sway over that. All of them were gone or would be soon.

What was left unsaid, undone were not only things from her past. They were also what was stretching out in front of her. Leaving meant not just leaving this behind, but going somewhere else, somewhere new.

In this moment, though, she was here, with the salty mist on her face, the waves and the gulls echoing in her ears, the sun shining too-bright into her eyes—those were not things any image, still or video or 3D, could capture. She would concentrate on the details now so that when she got to Mars or Titan or wherever they sent her, she could call them to mind and remember.

THIS AIN'T THE APOCA-RICH YOU HOPED FOR

Tuere T.S. Ganges

Mom used to yell at the TV about how unrealistic a show or movie was instead of turning the channel.

"Can you believe this?" She'd turn to my playpen. "No electricity in the apocalypse? Ed Begley Jr. rides a bike to power his toaster every morning! There's waterwheels and windmills. An apocalyptic event might knock out major power grids...yes...but these fools crying over the last freaking battery is ridiculous."

I was too young to understand what she meant...and honestly, I was too old to be in a fucking playpen...but mom yelled at her TV and I had all my favorite things in reach. It worked for us.

I had one teddy bear named Boomer. One doll named Angela. A pink, plastic football. A bucket of jumbo blocks. The book with the mosquito. The book with the caterpillar. The book with the little, brown princess. A sippy cup full of kiwi-strawberry juice. A yellow crescent moon pillow. And a multicolored blanket with satin edges. Everything was in its place around me to play with at my will.

Our puppy, Jumpman, couldn't get to anything. Neither could my little cousin on days when mom had to watch him. My playpen was off limits to everyone but me.

"Don't run now," mom yelled, "everybody knew them damn zombies was out on that side of the road but you just had to go look for some gold-plated lighter your daddy left ya when he died? Your dad's dead, you think he want you to have some lighter or you think he want you to live, fool?"

That's when she'd impart her apocalyptic wisdom my way. "So help me tah Gawd, Trini, I leave ya something when I die...you better drop whatever it is if it'll keep ya from gettin' eaten by some damn zombie... ya hear?"

I heard her. I didn't know what the heck she meant by any of it then, but I heard her. "Oooo-kay!" I was still adorable, and I knew it. I squeezed my fat fist together and threw it in the air with the same dedication my mom did when she raised a fist at other black people "doin' their thing," or "risin' up on these bastards."

When mom wasn't watching one version of the end of the world or another, she was on her laptop blogging about one version of the world ending or another. Or she'd be tinkering around the backyard or the screened-in patio with some self-sustaining, earth-saving project that would surely get us off-the-grid one day. She built a chicken coop for chickens she planned to get. She bought single solar panels that she planned to climb up on the roof with. She had a compost to dump the raked leaves in and a ceramic owl she hid dollar bills in. She stored canned food and bottled water in big plastic bins in the crawlspace under the house. Then one day, in the middle of whittling sharp points on the ends of broken branches that had fallen from the trees, she had her a-ha moment that would make us "apoca-rich!"

"Toilet paper, Trini! Toilet paper! All the books and movies got people bartering for cans of food and jugs of clean water...but somebody's gotta have the TP market on lock! Toilet paper and tampons, girlie! We're gonna be set when this fool in the White House finally piss off the wrong person and all hell breaks loose. Grab your backpack, I'm gonna find some coupons!"

By then, I was six. The only way my parents could get me to go to school was to assure me I'd still have all my stuff. My dad bought me a backpack that was almost as big as I was. He tipped my playpen on its side and let me pack my favorite things. A year and a half later, the house was playpen-free and I didn't go anywhere without my stuff. My stuff was more sophisticated then. I was over the pink football, the pillow, the blanket. I had more books and logical necessities like tissues, bandages, dental floss, an umbrella, and a flashlight.

"Nia, what the hell?" Dad yelled when he got home. The living room had 30 supersized cases of toilet paper plus 10 econo-packs of tampons. We were one broken refrigerator and an overflowing litterbox of catshit shy from an episode of Hoarders.

Mom's face lit up. "We're going to be Apoca-rich!" Her toothy smile stretched her painted-red lips across the creamy cocoa-ness of her skin. Her brown, braided hair was wrapped up in the colorful cloth, coiled into a cotton crown atop her head. She was stunning.

Dad's slightly lighter brown face was wrinkled at the sides of his nose and across the forehead. He was angry. He yanked the knit cap off of his head and the thick locks of his hair fell beyond his shoulders like an octopus who'd just given up.

They had the worst argument I'd ever witnessed. It took a while before they heard me crying and moved the wall of toilet paper I'd built around me long before my dad ever got home. He stopped talking and held me in his arms. Then he kissed my forehead and left. The divorce didn't come right away, but it happened. The wild thing is that mom didn't want to give up her stuff, but she couldn't afford the house on her own. She lost her marriage and her stuff. I learned not to hold onto anything you couldn't fit in a backpack.

•   •   •

"Trini, what should we do?"

I was straddling my bike in the middle of my tribe, as I called them. I was almost 17, tall, skinny, and bow-legged in my cut-off denim shorts and shredded M.I.A. concert t-shirt. My hair was pulled back into one cloud of an afro puff, and I bit on my full, bottom lip to keep it from quivering because all of these people looked to me for answers and, at the moment, my take on our situation wasn't too hopeful.

Long story short: mom was right. The fool in the White House pissed off the wrong person and all hell broke loose. Mom, who wound up working for the government to make enough money to take care of us, was killed in an explosion when a patriot drove himself into the federal building she was in. I stayed with dad for a year, then he was imprisoned for delivering newspapers, which was his night job. The news source he worked for had been added to the list of "anti-American propaganda-makers" that morning. He rarely read that paper, he was always working. Of course, that didn't matter. He'd been awaiting sentencing for four years when a prison riot broke out and he was trampled to death. When he was first arrested, I had to move out to the country with my grandparents. I kept waiting to hear that dad was released and I could go home, but a different call came.

"Well," I looked down the road we'd all pedaled, "we already know what's that way." The insane civil war that erupted between the conservatives and the liberals resulted in a lot of burnt-out buildings and makeshift roadblocks. Then, when the conservatives and the liberals realized the 1% was sitting back and counting money while the poor folks fought, they banded together against the rich. And wouldn't you know it? The 1% controlled the real army and the real power grids and the real Internet and airwaves. They shut everything down, built walls around their mansions, and took their private jets to Europe or some elite tropical island.

People who lived in rural areas like my grandparents thought they'd be fine. They grew their own food and enjoyed playing board games by candlelight. I used my mother's tutelage to prepare for the day looters would show up. The way I saw it, people in the closest city would exhaust all of their resources in a year and would consider venturing out for places where people had fresh food. Money was useless, so if they came across someone who wasn't interested in trading things, they'd probably take what they wanted and pray for forgiveness later. I began to train my friends in ways to hide out, hoard things, and hit back if all else failed.

We lasted a couple of years with minor battles but then came the gang. They rolled at least 40-deep, wearing blue jeans and hiking boots. At first glance, one would think they were some kind of scout group without a distinct uniform. They sang friendly songs from almost-forgotten pop radio stations' playlists. When they got to my cousin Sauce's house, the leader smiled at my aunt and asked if she had anything to trade.

"I'm Justin," the leader said, with his blonde hair pulled up into a bun, "that there is my girlfriend, Gina"—a friendly-looking redhead waved—"and he's my brother, James." He thumbed at a man who looked like a taller version of himself. James only nodded without smiling. The leader explained that all the other people were from his neighborhood in the city and they didn't have a lot of food left. "But we have some things that might be worth something to you and maybe we can trade ya."

Well, Sauce got his nickname from being my aunt Imani's favorite taste tester for all the sauces she'd made. When the 1% blew up the main power plants to blind the world to their exodus, aunt Imani finally listened to me about the need to stock up on food and resources for the day when bartering would be our only currency. She'd already had a load of mason jars full of spaghetti sauce, apple sauce, soups, stews, and gravies; however, she got to work on extra stuff while she still had propane.

"What ya got to trade?" She asked Justin.

Justin smiled again and beckoned for Gina to join him on my aunt's porch. "Gina, show this nice lady your jewelry."

Gina pulled a velvet bag out of her knapsack and showed her some necklaces and earrings.

"Well, I don't have much use for jewelry these days," my aunt said. "But since you guys are in need, I will take those green earrings for a case of soup. I got 20 jars in a box. That should help you and your friends." My aunt smiled politely. Sauce and I were watching by the windows from the front corners of her living room and I could tell her smile was forced. Aunt Imani never did have a poker face.

I tilted my head to see Sauce on the other side. He was the closest to her and he had one of grandpa's shotguns. I raised one finger, our symbol to get ready, and he nodded.

"Well, that is nice, miss!" Justin said. "You need me to come in and get that heavy box for you?"

Gina fumbled with the foam that held the emerald earrings. It distracted me, and it distracted her. Both of us missed Justin pull a handgun from behind and aim it for my aunt's face.

"Oh my—" was all my aunt could say. I ran towards her and Sauce punched through the side window with the tip of the shotgun, but it wasn't enough to stop Justin from shooting my aunt point blank.

"No!" I yelled as I caught Aunt Imani before she hit the floor. She and my mother looked so much alike. I wondered if my mom's face was just as peaceful before the bomb went off.

Sauce fired a round that hit Gina in her chest. Justin barged in and aimed the gun at me. Sauce pulled the shotgun in and shot Justin in the arm. He dropped his handgun and stumbled back out onto the porch.

"The door!" I yelled for Sauce. He pushed it shut and threw the deadbolt.

"Ma!" he screamed. Unfortunately, there was no need. My aunt was gone and a small army was outside.

"They'll shoot through the door next, Sauce. We gotta go." I grabbed Justin's gun that landed near Aunt Imani's feet.

Sauce picked up his mother and swung her over his shoulder. He was two years younger than I was, but a whole head taller. Aunt Imani's weight didn't seem to register as any kind of strain on him physically. The pain was all in his face. He motioned for me to grab the box of ammo he'd left on the window ledge and we started to hustle on out to the backyard.

My aunt had let Sauce and I build a bit of a fort in the crawlspace under the back porch of their house back when she thought I was just as silly as her sister, my mom, for preparing for the worst. Sauce put her on the little air mattress we'd put in the corner and I pushed the old stainless steel refrigerator door we'd found over the thin wooden door that was already a part of the house.

Next, I grabbed a walkie-talkie, and started to click our situation in Morse code. My tribe of believers all had walkies on the same station and we'd taught ourselves enough Morse code to know what to do when we heard it. Above us, Justin and his gang were shooting. When the shooting stopped, we could hear his muffled commands to "check upstairs" and "grab what you can." Every now and then he'd shriek, "Gina! They killed Gina!" and then something would crash, which I assumed was him breaking things like picture frames and my aunt's knick-knacks.

A few responses to my call trickled in. Most acknowledged that the message was received and that help would arrive soon. Our plan was that if ever an alert like this one was sent, the tribe would come together for a bigger defense. They needed to get their weapons and ammo, which was mostly hunting stuff like shotguns, crossbows, and knives, but Yoshi, who was black and never stepped foot in Asia, had a few samurai swords from his Japanophile collection. They would meet at someone's house, get on their bikes to head our way, then watch from a distance to figure out what they were working with. Sauce and I pulled together our arms: bullets for the shotgun, water balloons filled with vinegar or ammonia, pepper spray, a kitchen knife, and a baseball bat. Justin's gun was only missing a few rounds. Outside, we had a few boobie traps that could slow a small mob down, but if all those people had guns like I figured, we were in trouble.

Taps and pauses came through on my walkie that told me my tribe was in position. A moment later, a message came through to suggest we stay still until they sent an all clear. Sauce shook his head. He wanted to go find Justin and kill him with his bare hands. I mouthed, "No. Wait."

Next we heard a siren. Considering we'd run out of gasoline months ago and the local sheriff had left before that, I knew it was Beatbox, my girlfriend, making the sound into her cheerleader megaphone.

"Go-go-go!" I heard overhead. Heavy footsteps and noises of objects being dragged, followed.

Once everything was silent, Beatbox's amplified voice came over my walkie. "You guys okay?"

"Yeah, babe," I replied. I would save the news about my aunt for face-to-face time.

I coaxed Sauce to follow me out into the sunlight. "We need help to bury her." We thought about checking the house but decided we weren't ready.

We grabbed clean shirts off of the clothesline and changed in silence. "Let's check in with the tribe and then go see grandma." Sauce nodded and we jumped on our bikes to meet up with the rest.

Justin's gang came back the next day, a little sooner than I expected. They were more careful about choosing houses with people who were home alone, but they killed three more people and cleaned out their supplies of food. Beatbox's great-grandfather was one of the victims. Her sobbing voice broke the news over our station. I left our small funeral for my aunt just as Sauce began to cover his mother with dirt in grandma's backyard.

I met Beatbox in one of the hunting perches her great-grandfather had on the edge of his property. With binoculars, we watched Justin and the others make themselves at home. It was clear they'd claimed the land as their own. Considering they killed and looted from others, it was safe to say they'd keep going until they'd claimed the entire town.

"It's what I'd do if I was a greedy bastard," I whispered to Beatbox who didn't understand why Justin did what he did. "There will always be some greedy fuckers who think they need to take anything and everything. This Justin guy probably ran some business, thought he was one of the 1% and was shocked to find out he wasn't. He made himself the head honcho in his corner of the city, only, what could he produce that others would need to bow down at his feet for? Not much. He needs to be in control. Your Pop-pop has a nice piece of land. He has goats and chickens, as well. I doubt they even found the pond yet." I stopped to think. "You know what? He's expecting the 1% to come back. That's why he's taking things like jewelry. He thinks that when they come back, he'll have to be accepted as one of them if he's made himself the new one-percenter."

Beatbox nodded. Her hazel eyes were full of tears and sorrow. I watched her grieve. Was she thinking about fun times with her great-grandfather? The times they spent fishing in the pond, the days of her chasing the animals while he watched and laughed at her little legs and big determination? Now, I could see her asking without asking, what did she have left of him?

I brushed her wavy, black hair out of her face. "As long as you're breathing and can remember him, your Pop-pop is alive. Do you understand?" It's what my father told me about my mother when I wanted to bring all of her possessions with me to his small apartment after she died. It's what I reminded myself when my grandmother handed me the phone to let me hear for myself about what happened to my dad. Everything I had left of my parents was seen in the mirror or felt when I put my hand to my heart. It would take time for Sauce and Beatbox to understand after their great losses, but I was living testimony that it would be enough.

We climbed down the tree and met up with the tribe near my aunt's fresh grave. The timing sucked, but I had to inform them, "I don't think we can beat this Justin guy and his gang."

"What do you mean?" Yoshi asked.

"They aren't here to grab some stuff and go. They're a fucking alien invasion. They're here to take over."

Beatbox nodded. "They killed my great-grandfather. They basically moved into his house."

"What?" I didn't realize my grandma had come back outside. "What are you talking about?"

"Grandma." I looked to Sauce and back. "My mom wasn't crazy. I don't know what else has to happen before you guys will take me seriously, but the apocalypse is here. Hollywood had everybody thinking it would be aliens or a bunch of synchronized earthquakes, but no. The enemy is a regular man who thinks he's entitled to take whatever he wants and right now, he wants our town."

"What would anyone want with our town?"

Sauce kneeled over his mother's grave and traced his fingers across the soil. "Grandma, they just want. It doesn't matter what. My mother offered to give them a case of soup and he shot her." He put his hand over his eyes. "We didn't want to tell you, but I shot and killed one of them. Do you know what this guy did? He kept looting."

Our grandmother drew her hand to her mouth with a gasp but didn't say anything for some time. Finally, her words cut through the silence. "I'm getting too old to be hiking or riding a bike."

My nose started to burn as my eyes blurred with tears. I'd thought about this, too. Grandma was only in her 60's. She wasn't one of the yoga-grannies that could run marathons back when people cared about that stuff, but she wasn't using a walker either. I'd tried to get her out on her bicycle again. I'd talked to her about escape routes. I figured I had to at least plant plans in her mind so that she could fend for herself if she ever had to. Grandpa's stroke left him in a wheelchair. His speech was slurred but he'd already told me that we should just leave him behind if shit got real.

"All I wan' is my Bi-ble an' a bul-let," he struggled to say. He had a revolver. I made sure he had it handy that morning. His Bible was where it always was, on the piano between photos of him and grandma at their wedding, and my mom and aunt in a pile of colorful leaves.

"Grandma, Sauce and I stocked up your basement a while ago. We can help get grandpa down there and show you how to lock yourselves in. I think if we get over to the next town, we can prepare them for when Justin wants to expand his territory. Maybe they'll listen. We can get a safe place and come back for you two."

Grandma kept my gaze until it sunk in that I was serious. As the realization set into her face it was as though she aged 10 years right in front of my eyes. Denial was over, the apocalypse was real, and it had taken both of her daughters. She glanced at Sauce and back to me. This might be the last time she'd see her grandchildren. "Okay." She nodded slowly. "Okay."

My tribe helped to get my grandfather down into the basement. They left Sauce and me there to show our grandparents how to crank the rechargeable flashlights and battery kits. We put the alphabet in Morse code by the spare walkie-talkie and taught grandma how it would sound if we tapped "I love you" to her. For the two of them, they had enough food and water to last for over a month. The worse part was they'd have to use a toilet we'd fashioned from a broken lawn chair and 5-gallon buckets. They'd have to pour in strong cleaners with bleach or ammonia (never both) and put a lid over it until it was full. Then use another one. We had 12 empty containers in the basement ready to go.

"Hopefully, you'll be able to move around the house, go outside and everything for a while before Justin's gang gets out this way." I didn't trust it but prayed they were done looting houses. Sauce and I took turns hugging her. I ran up to get grandpa's Bible and put it on his lap. I kissed his forehead and fought back my tears so he'd have a lasting image of me being strong.

Meanwhile, the rest of the tribe was doing similar things. Letting their families know about what had gone down and figuring out what to do next. We planned to meet up on the edge of town away from where Justin had set up camp. I checked my backpack to make sure it was stocked for the next journey and chuckled to myself at the compressed roll of toilet paper I squeezed into an outer pocket. "This ain't the apoca-rich you'd hoped for, ma." Of course, she would want me to leave the econo-buy toilet paper stash if it would save me from a swarm of brain-hungry zombies, but I still worried I didn't have enough of anything.

Sauce and I got on our bikes and met the rest. Everyone looked to me for direction. Mom had only taught me how to stock and store like giant squirrels preparing for the craziest winter ever. I'd added knowledge on with some self-defense classes, learned how to hike and survive in the woods, and I knew how to plant stuff if it was up to me to replenish the planet. I didn't know what to do in the middle. Where was I supposed to lead them? Were we supposed to kill and loot like Justin and his gang, too? What if the next town saw us as the enemy?

"Well, we already know what's that way," I said pointing down the road into town. "As sure as I knew people like Justin were coming, I'm sure they'll keep coming. Not many wanted to hear me before, but now we know what's to come. Now we know we need to warn the next town over. We can take notes from the one-percenters before they bounced and build some roadblocks with an armed crew on watch. Hopefully, we can save the next town. Hopefully, we can come back to our homes and live peacefully again." I shrugged. "The one thing we know we can do for sure is to ride on."

I turned my bike in the direction we'd be going and set my right foot on its pedal. Sauce positioned himself on my left as Beatbox rolled over to my right. I forced hopeful smiles and nodded to each. "So be it. Get to it," I said with purpose and pushed off for the next town and whatever we'd meet along the way.

THIS DUSTY WAY TO GALAXIES BEYOND

Julia K. Patt

Raena wakes an hour earlier than she must. Already she has to rise well before the sun to pack the cart and begin the long ride around the Drytown markets.

But the hour before that, this hour, is hers. This is when the launches happen.

She wiggles out of the bed without rousing her adopted siblings, a scraggly group of eight orphans the fruit sellers have plucked from all over Drytown. The room smells like them, their dusty hair and baby breath and the sticky soles of their feet, still dark with berry juice.

She would sleep on the outer edge of the room if she could, but Hiri and Nunks have trouble holding their bladders through the night and so they take priority. Raena hops carefully over Nunks' outstretched hand, then does a clumsy pirouette on her good foot around Hiri before she can escape.

She keeps her metal foot and hand in the hall outside to keep the littles away from them. The foot is especially heavy, made of recycled scrap metal, and a running little could easily trip over it and fall. It also makes it easier to slip out in the mornings.

Raena buckles the pieces onto her stumps, both on the right side—she still doesn't know why. She oils the joints carefully so they don't squeak, but it's impossible not to make that th-thump th-thump noise as she walks. Her prosthetics are ungainly, but they're all the fruit sellers can afford and she will not ask for more.

Outside, in the gray-blue night, she rides her cycle away from the little house and through the conical structures where the fruit grows, the vines and squat bushes and top-heavy trees greening the metal skeletons. In a few hours, when the sky lightens, the misters will start, letting the plants get their moisture before the risk of evaporation increases.

She pedals away from them and out of Drytown to the very limit of Tern, the great city on the edge of the desert. She looks out into the dark expanse, the stars still glittering down, the planet's seven moons shining bright. The massive field of solar panels is still dormant, so it's easy to see the bright orange lights of the launch station out there on the Travelers' Plateau.

Raena stands, holding her breath, quietly counting down. When she hits one, a flash of light explodes on the horizon; then it ascends upupupup and away from Tern into the near-morning sky. Another team flying out into the nothing, to see what they can find among the stars beyond. What she wouldn't give to join them, one day, foolish as it feels to dream.

She cannot afford to dawdle, but she pedals as slowly as time will allow on the way home, her mind's eye tracking the arc of the rocket into space.

·   ·   ·

The fruit sellers are awake and waiting for her with breakfast when she returns. She knows not all of them approve, but they voted a while back and the majority see no harm in her hobby, as they call it.

They have made her the usual fortified protein porridge today with a generous portion of stewed fruit over the top to cut the meal's musty flavor. Neither she nor the littles have tired of the fruit yet; it is still novel to be able to eat as much as you want of something—well, the bruised and unsightly specimens anyway—and all of the children have gone over plump in the year since they were adopted.

There are always some fruit sellers to see her off in the mornings. A collective of seven, they send most of their wares to the Waterside markets and restaurants, but they save a portion to sell to their own neighborhoods in Drytown, where the fruit is an important source of hydration. So while planting, cultivation, picking, and packing falls to the collective and the littles, Raena has her own unique job of taking a cart full of fruit to the markets every day.

Outside, the fruit sellers help her hitch the fully loaded and secured cart to her cycle and steady it as she climbs onto the seat, making sure her metal foot locks into place. They've attached her saddlebags, full of lunch and precious water-buds—succulent pods bursting with moisture. One of them, Gorse, pats her on the head before she departs.

"Blessings go with you, child," he murmurs.

· · ·

The morning market is uneventful. She sells most of the spiny fruit early because they bruise easily and tend to look pulpy and brown by the end of the day otherwise. The berries never last for the midday market; expensive as they are, the few bunches she carries almost always vanish right away. Parked between Queemy, who sells nuts, and Loola, who does spices, she can do a brisk business and does.

Here, in the heart of Drytown, it's hard to image the rest of the city, luminous and green with its stories of thriving gardens and the reviving breezes from the bay and the sea beyond. Tern itself is a bright crescent hugging the water, with Drytown clinging to its back like a sick, thirsty child. The original settlers were the builders who constructed the solar fields; some of those stayed with their families, unable to find more work, but mostly the poor and indigent moved into their abandoned shelters, making what was meant to be temporary something permanent. Now, Drytown keeps growing but can't expand beyond the solar fields, so little shacks pile up and up, stretching towards the sky in a dusty imitation of Tern's platinum towers.

Raena rides her cycle with its somewhat lightened load to the midday market, which stands closest to the city median, the boundary between Drytown and the rest of Tern. There's no fence or tangible boundary between the two, and yet the people of Drytown are as fully separated by the dividing line as they would be by a one hundred-foot wall. Beyond, the buildings might be shabby by Tern standards, but in Drytown they would be coveted palaces.

Raena takes a corner where she can best look into the city, and more than one customer catches her daydreaming. She's thinking about the Needle Tower, where the space travelers train, only a few miles from here. Old Jex, one of her regulars, waves a hand in front of her face.

"Never really with us are you, Raena," he says, not unkindly, and drops his money into her metal palm. "Wishing don't make it so. Better settle."

"Better settle" is something of an unofficial motto among Drytowners. She hates it. She hates that when they look at her, they see a damaged child with little chance at a future. Without the fruit sellers she'd be a beggar, no doubt, fat little cripple, they say, as if she doesn't deserve their care. Those full cheeks would sink, that round belly collapse.

One time, a group of boys kicked her bike out from under her in the midday market and they all laughed, even the adults, while she was pinned under it, trying to disengage her metal foot from the pedal. There are better worlds than these, she tells herself often, but she doesn't know if she will ever reach them.

She's giving Jex his change when a murmur goes through the market. There, in the sky above Tern, is a plume of bright blue smoke. Excitement grips Raena's stomach. A new space traveler has completed their training.

·   ·   ·

She listens to the wireless with the littles that evening after dinner and nighttime chores. Aura Mayana is the newest space traveler to clear her testing protocols, even though she's only been training a few months. She'll go up in the launch with Ersten Yong and Joedi Blaze in three weeks.

"They're having a parade for her!" Raena tells the fruit sellers after, when the littles are getting ready for bed. "It's going to include Drytown, too. People will want snacks—shouldn't I bring the cart?"

The fruit sellers exchange looks. They came to Drytown not for wealth but to care for green and growing things. They sell their wares in order to survive, but Raena knows they are not very business-minded, for all that everyone, including her and the littles, calls them the fruit sellers. Gorse, whom the others particularly respect, is a member of a religious order which dictates he live among the needy. All of them share similar philosophies.

"Please," she begs. "Everyone else will raise their prices. We can at least sell water-buds so that people don't get dehydrated. It will do some good, I promise."

Gorse strokes his beard. "It's for you, too, isn't it? So you can see this woman, this Aura Mayana, who will go to space?"

Raena nods, worried he will chastise her for being selfish.

"See that you do not forget to actually sell some fruit." His dark eyes crinkle at the corners as he takes in her smile, her excitement.

·   ·   ·

The parade route winds around the perimeter of Drytown until it turns down the street where the evening market usually sets up, the widest road back into Tern. Raena rides her cycle to the corner of this street and converts the cart into a stand with more enthusiasm than she has ever mustered. The littles wanted to come with her to work today, but Gorse and the others said they would have to make do with hearing Raena's stories. "As will we," he added, winking at her.

It is early, but already people have begun to gather at the parade route. As the crowd grows, she begins to worry that she won't be able to see much. Her foot drags and scrapes as she climbs up on a concrete block next to her cart. There, she can see the street and keep track of her wares. Already, she spots some urchins weaving through the crowds, dipping their nimble fingers into bags and pockets. Raena squeezes the money pouch around her neck for reassurance. She'll give the thieving children some leftover fruit at the end of the day at the fruit sellers' direction, but she doesn't have to trust them.

It's nearly midday before the shouts and rumble of engines announce the parade's approach. No one in Drytown—indeed, no one in most of Tern—owns mechanized transport except for the city government, and even they must be discrete with their fuel usage or face extreme criticism and recalls. The space travelers, however, are worth it, and Raena sees her first glimpse of them standing in the back of a squat flatbed truck and waving.

In her excitement—is that Aura Mayana in the front? Is she getting down from the truck?—she loses track of the cart for a moment, moving her steadying medal hand so she can get a better look at the figures on the truck. That's when it happens: a small tussle breaks out in the crowd as people fight to see. One of the combatants crashes back into the little cart, overturning the whole thing and scattering fruit everywhere.

"No, no!" Raena cries as grapes and spiny fruit get crushed underfoot around her. Abandoning her cycle and toppled cart, she goes scuttling into the street after some rolling apples, snatching them up and stuffing them into her pockets as she's able. There's a commotion and the sound of a truck horn. Certain she's going to be hit, Raena extends her metal hand in what defense it can offer—and then she's crouching nose to nose with Aura Mayana.

The traveler, seeing the mess, has bent down to retrieve an apple. Now she straightens, impossibly tall as the travelers always seem to be. Maybe they need those long limbs to pilot the ships? But unlike Ersten Yong and Joedi Blaze, who stand behind her looking bemused, the newest traveler is not lithe and fine-boned, but heavyset and round-faced.

"Hello," she says to Raena a little shyly. "Are you alright? We seem to have made a mess."

"It's fine," Raena says, still staring. "I should have kept hold of the cart."

There's a murmur up ahead, people wondering why everything's stopped, and then a man with a stunner comes back to check on them. "Are you okay here, Mz?" he asks. "We really ought to keep going."

"Just a moment, please," the space traveler says. "Ersten, Joedi, some help?" And the three of them in their shining, silvery jumpsuits step into the crowd to retrieve Raena's cycle and cart, the latter now dented on one side, the former bent at the front wheel. Raena and Aura Mayana deposit what fruit they could recover into the cart. But it's now irreparably dusty and bruised—she can't sell fruit like that and looking at it makes Raena want to cry.

"Where are your folks?" Aura Mayana asks once they've put everything to rights, as much as they're able anyway. Ersten and Joedi regard her with good-natured patience while the guard stutters again that they should keep going. "Or—are you alone?"

Raena shakes her head. "They're…" Well, it's complicated, isn't it? "My family lives out by the solar fields," she explains. "We grow fruit," she adds unnecessarily and winces.

Aura Mayana laughs. "So I see. Well, we'd be remiss if we didn't see you home, wouldn't we? What's your name?"

"Raena," she whispers, but Aura Mayana hears her perfectly.

"Raena," she repeats.

Her name, in the mouth of someone who will travel among the stars.

·   ·   ·

She can't imagine what the fruit sellers must be thinking as the rumbling flatbed truck approaches the little house. They're taking a break from the midday heat with the littles, passing around water-buds and fallen fruit. When the truck pulls into the yard, they jump up. Gorse and the other adults rush forward, lifting Raena, her cycle, and the battered cart out of the back. They're already peppering her with questions—"What happened? Are you hurt? Did someone do this?"—when Aura Mayana swings down from the passenger side and approaches them. The fruit sellers fall into silence, staring. If her shining uniform didn't give her away, the space traveler's emblem on her collar surely did, a rocket arcing into the stars.

"There was a small incident. Entirely our fault, I assure you. We didn't anticipate we'd draw such a large crowd in Drytown," she says, taking the fruit sellers' hands one by one. "Hello, I'm Aura Mayana."

"Well, we know, of course. We're the Drytown Collective," Gorse tells her, which is what the fruit sellers call themselves. "Thank you for bringing Raena home...can we offer you something eat?"

The travelers look around at each other and shrug. The guard makes a small, frustrated noise, but says nothing. "That would be lovely," Aura Mayana says. "Thank you."

·   ·   ·

Which is how three space travelers happen to be sitting in the fruit sellers' yard with Raena and the littles, the littles bouncing around and peppering them with questions. How does the rocket work? Are they scared to go into space? Excited? What color are the stars? Where will they go?

"Okay, okay," the fruit sellers tell them after the umpteenth question. "It is time for afternoon rest. Upstairs, please, and give us a moment's peace."

For a moment, Raena is sure they will send her to lie down with the littles, but they don't. Her siblings troop away in a chorus of groans while the travelers laugh and wave to them.

"It's amazing you've been able to take in so many," Ersten Yong tells Gorse. "Are they all from Drytown?"

"All except our Raena here," her guardian replies. "The orphanage found her at the ports in Waterside when she was an infant. They think a stowaway must have brought her to Tern, but we don't know much more than that."

"Ah, a fellow traveler," Aura Mayana smiles down at Raena.

She's never heard this version of her story before; the orphanage at the city median makes up her earliest memories. The caretakers there never made it sound like she came from anywhere but Drytown; most orphans come from Drytown.

"Your own travels begin soon, don't they?" Gorse asks. "Where does your mission take you?"

"The Goatherder Nebula. It's a funny name, isn't it? It's amazing what our astronomers find in the cosmos…and what they decide to call them."

The adults sit and talk more about the mission, about the traveler programs and how long they spend in the stasis before they can journey among the stars, collecting samples and data for Tern back home. Aura Mayana is a pilot, so she will spend the journey in a half-suspended state, a kind of lucid dreaming.

"Quite a sacrifice," Gorse murmurs.

"It is taxing, yes," Joedi Blaze agrees. "That's why they only pick the toughest candidates as pilots. You need an exact combination of hardiness and mental acuity to do it." Her voice brims with pride, rather than envy, as she talks about her teammate.

Aura Mayana blushes. "Really, Joedi, as if being a science officer on a spaceship is anything to sneer at."

Joedi shrugs. Her skin is darker than Gorse's, and Raena remembers vaguely that Joedi Blaze is originally from the Southern Coast, many hundreds of miles from Tern. "Not that I ever doubted you, even after the accident."

"Joedi," Aura Mayana warns. "You know we're not supposed to talk about that."

The other traveler rolls her eyes. "These are smart people, Aura. They understand that the traveler program has its risks. Besides…" she nods at Raena, an exaggerated gesture. "The kid might like to know."

Aura Mayana looks at Raena for a long moment. Her face is thoughtful. Finally, she reaches down and rolls up one silvery pant leg. There's a neat, almost surgical looking scar at her knee. Below that, there's not skin, but a fleshy silicone.

Raena stares.

"Everyone thinks I just started the traveler program, but the truth is I only just came back to it a few months ago. I've been rehabilitating. We had a simulation that didn't…didn't go so well."

"Aura's been training and getting back into condition for about a year now," Ersten explains. "She was originally in our traveler cohort, which is why we're so glad she finished in time to join us as our pilot. She's one of the best there is, you know."

Aura Mayana blushes again and shakes her head. She reaches down to take Raena's good hand and squeezes, just once.

The guard appears at the edge of the yard, looking pointedly at his watch and clearing his throat. Gorse gets to his feet. "I suppose we've kept you for long enough," he says.

"Not at all." Ersten shakes his hand. "Thank you for your hospitality. Your home is beautiful—so full of life."

"I'm glad we got to see some of the real Drytown," Joedi agrees. "We'll tell the others how many supporters we have here."

Aura Mayana only says, "Thank you all," before the three of them follow the guard back to the truck. But Raena can still feel the warmth of her hand on hers, long after they leave.

· · ·

It's the talk of the neighborhood for months, how the space travelers came to visit the fruit sellers and broke bread with them. The adults smile at the silly rumors, but they're happy to distribute more of their wares to the curious. More food and clothing for the littles.

It doesn't help the gossip that about a week after the incident a replacement cycle arrives for Raena, shiny and brand new, with a two-wheeled cart that hitches to the back. With it are a set of data discs and a note from Aura Mayana: better start studying now. The discs are comprehensive: physics, astronomy, chemistry, engineering, advanced calculus. Everything you need to know to travel the stars. She'll get the littles started in their learning, too, she decides.

The night before the next launch, Raena can barely sleep. She's up well before she needs to leave and slips down the stairs, no longer so pained by the sound of the th-thunk, th-thunk of her scrap metal foot. Once she learns enough, she can build and design her own; this is a temporary measure and she appreciates the fruit sellers and their efforts.

Her new cycle practically flies to the edge of the solar fields, the desert beyond as cool and gray as an alien world. She waits in the dark, half-dreaming of her own ascendance to the top of the traveler rockets, just her and the steady tide of her own breath in her suit, the journey's way seared into her memory as surely as her own neighborhood. The seconds tick down and the explosion of jet fuel seems especially bright as it lifts Aura Mayana and her crew up and into the air, through the atmosphere, and to the stars beyond.

Someday, Raena knows, she will follow them.

ACCIDENT

Gretchin Lair

I t was a horrible accident, but Katrina couldn't stop smiling. Her bike was tangled in the intersection and her left arm hurt sharply whenever she moved. But she felt euphoric, a bright bloom of relief and release in her chest. Hopefully she had miscarried. Everything was going to be all right.

"Oh, god, I'm so sorry. Are you okay?" The driver's long red hair blew across her face. Her hazard lights were on and the door was open, creating a lee as other cars crawled around them. Katrina continued to smile and nod as she let the driver help her onto the curb and retrieve her bike from the road.

"Oh, god," the driver repeated. "Do you want me to call an ambulance?"

Katrina's adrenaline was fading, and with it, her mood dulled. She shook her head. Her short braids bounced against her neck. "No, I'm okay." She tried to flex her arm and winced. "We don't have insurance, anyway." She wanted to take off her helmet, but it seemed like too much trouble. She was so tired.

"I'm sorry," the driver said. "I'm Heather. I can take you home if you want. I have a bike rack. Or is there someone we can call?"

Suddenly things snapped back into focus. Her husband was watching the girls. Katrina's stomach sank as she realized she was probably going to be down for a couple of days. Kevin wasn't going to like that much.

She checked herself over. Nothing seemed like it couldn't wait until she could see a doctor. The sunny day that had made the ride irresistible had been replaced with thick clouds, and she shivered in her thin bike shorts and T-shirt.

So Katrina crawled into the back seat and gave Heather directions to her house. Numbly, she knew she should be more cautious with a stranger. But she didn't think Heather was a threat, and she knew calling Kevin would be a big hassle. He'd have to call someone to watch the girls or pack them up when he came to get her. She'd be waiting there forever. She just wanted to go home.

As Heather pulled away from the intersection, Katrina tried to make herself comfortable between the child seats. But she didn't see any toys or spills, so she asked, "How many kids do you have?"

"Oh, uh, none, really," Heather said, guiltily. "I'm not married. I'm helping to take care of my nieces and nephews. My sister died a few months ago." From the rear-view mirror, Katrina saw a shadow fall over Heather's eyes.

"Oh, I'm so sorry," Katrina murmured, not knowing what else to say.

"It's okay."

They drove in silence. The motion of the car made Katrina sleepy. She could tell Heather was trying to drive carefully, easing over bumps and avoiding sharp turns. She watched the streets pass: a blur of stores with "Help Wanted" signs, mothers walking their children to playgrounds in big groups, more elementary schools being built. She felt like she was floating, equal parts exhausted and ebullient, her skin tingling.

"Is your stomach okay?" Heather asked nervously, her eyes flicking between the rearview mirror and the road.

"Oh, yes," Katrina smiled as she realized she had been absentmindedly rubbing it. "It was just a close call," she said a little dreamily, still looking out the window.

Heather's eyes grew wide. "Oh, shit! Are you pregnant?" She looked horrified.

"What?" Katrina moved her arm quickly away from her stomach, trying to hide her guilt and surprise. "Whoah! No! I just meant we had a close call, that's all! Why would you even ask that?" Katrina made a face, leaned back in the seat and closed her eyes, ending the conversation. Heather mumbled an apology.

When they arrived at the house, Katrina stayed in the car as Heather knocked on her door. And then Kevin was there, and then the girls were there, and they were all talking at once and walking into the house while trying to avoid the toys on the floor and the boxes still stacked everywhere and the cereal spilled in the hall, and she heard words like "insurance" and "911" and "sorry" and "mommy."

She sat on the couch, leaning against a pile of laundry, carefully cradling her arm. She felt completely overwhelmed. She tried to smile reassuringly at everyone, especially at the girls—Amy had obviously been crying, and Jessie was loudly asking questions. Kevin was trying to keep the girls from pouncing on her while at the same time trying to talk to Heather. He was clearly angry but staying civil, and for that she was grateful.

After a while, Kevin took the girls to the kitchen, and Heather knelt by the couch.

"Hey," she said. "Since I've already got your bike, I'm just going to take it in to get fixed up, okay? I always get my stuff done at Jane's. They're great. Is that okay, or do you have another place you like to go?"

"No, we just moved here. That sounds fine."

"Oh, good!" Heather said. "Well, I mean, not good, obviously, but Jane's is a good place to know if you're new in town. It's a bike collective. They're really community minded. All women. They've helped me out a lot."

Katrina was surprised. "All women? Don't any of them have kids?"

"Oh, some of them, yeah. All the pre-school moms have work permits, though."

Heather wrote her phone number on the back of an envelope, using a pencil decorated with princesses. "Call me tomorrow after you get checked out and we'll talk about what to do next."

After Heather left, Katrina wanted to lie down, but her helmet was still on. She used her right hand to awkwardly unbuckle the clasp and push it off her head. She closed her eyes, trying to recapture that beautiful moment right after the accident.

·   ·   ·

The doctor tightened the sling. "Well, looks like you're going to be out of commission for a while," she said.

"How long?"

"At least ten weeks." The doctor was really a physician assistant. Her name, Paula, had been printed with label tape and stuck onto a CareFull Clinic plastic tag. It was slightly askew and thick with previous labels, but since she was wearing a white coat and had a stethoscope around her neck, it was hard not to think of her as a doctor.

"Ten weeks!" For the first time since the accident, Katrina felt like crying. How was she going to take care of two little girls for more than two months with a broken elbow?

Paula said, "Well, it could have been a lot worse, right?" She tapped on her handheld device. "Okay, I think you're good to go. I'll send the prescription to your pharmacy so you can pick it up on the way home."

Katrina didn't feel good to go, but she knew that was her signal to move along so the next person could be seen for stitches or kidney stones.

Still, she had to ask.

"Can something like this cause a miscarriage?" Katrina asked, as casually as she could.

"Oh, you're pregnant?" Paula asked, eyebrows raised. "You should have told me. That requires different reporting and assessment procedures. I'll have to order a pregnancy test." She turned to the screen and began tapping more boxes.

"No, no!" Katrina lied. "I mean, hypothetically, could something like this cause a miscarriage?"

Paula raised her head. "Well, it probably depends on gestational age. The earlier the pregnancy, the more likely the miscarriage."

Katrina hoped that was true. She wished she could just buy a pregnancy test at the grocery store, but she couldn't risk it. Instead, she asked: "Hypothetically, how would someone know they had miscarried?"

Paula looked at her a moment. "Hypothetically, I'd have them take a pregnancy test. But... you're approved for birth control, right?" She started tapping through screens again.

Katrina kept her face blank, trying to read Paula's expression. "We... lost track of it during the move. My husband hasn't applied for it in this state yet. We had an... accident," Katrina said carefully.

Paula took a beat, and her fingers stopped tapping. Without lifting her head, she said quietly, "If you need a pregnancy test in this clinic, I would need to send the results to the state. I'm a mandatory reporter. If you've had a miscarriage, you'll be scheduled for a home visit."

She looked up at Katrina, who blanched.

Paula smiled a little. "But hypothetically, if you aren't experiencing pregnancy symptoms, then a test wouldn't be necessary, would it? So, before you go, I need to ask you a few more questions about your arm to make sure we aren't missing anything serious. Are you experiencing nausea?"

"No," Katrina said, pleased to realize she hadn't felt any since the accident. Biking was one of the few things that helped with her morning sickness, which was why Kevin had offered to watch the girls.

"Increased urination? Fatigue? Heartburn? Constipation? Breast tenderness?"

Katrina shook her head at all of these.

"Then I think your arm is fine," Paula said, her face impassive, her tone clear. "But with a bad accident like that, sometimes symptoms can be delayed. If you notice cramping, bleeding or back pain, those might be signs of a more serious condition. I'll give you some materials and handouts to take home."

Katrina left the clinic with several sheets of paper, a white paper bag, and a hopeful heart.

•　　　•　　　•

"Ten weeks!" Kevin said. He was in the guest bedroom, packing a suitcase for another trip. He ran his hands through his sandy hair. He needed a haircut, but she liked it like this, a little softer than his usual business bristle. "But I can't take time off work! Even if I could take the time, we still have all the doctor bills to pay. And we don't have long before the baby comes."

Kevin never panicked. It was one of the reasons she loved him and almost certainly how they had managed to survive two difficult pregnancies and moving across the country. But his gaze was fixed between the suitcase and the wall, almost holding his breath, and she saw suddenly how tightly he was clinging to the edge, how determined he was to keep them all afloat, and it broke her heart.

"Kevin, I lost the baby," she said.

Kevin took a breath, his eyes wide. "Oh, Katrina," he said, sitting down beside her on the bed, looking stunned. "Thank goodness!" He smiled, almost laughing with relief. She smiled, too. She knew the feeling.

"I mean, of course, we would have gotten through it," he said. "This just gives us a little more breathing room after the move. I thought I was going to have to look for another job."

"You never said that!" She took his hand. "I sometimes wish we were born a little earlier, you know? When you could still... I mean, I love our kids, and I would have loved this one, but it would have been great if we could have..." She let the sentence drift.

"Well, yeah," Kevin said. "I guess I've got to apply for birth control again then."

"Definitely. Can you do it as soon as you get back?" Katrina said. "Please?" She hated how she sounded when she had to ask.

"Sure, yeah." He stood up and started packing again. "Well, there are no accidents, right? Everything happens for a reason."

He paused, a shirt dangling in his hand. "So maybe we should talk about having another kid—on purpose this time. We just barely squeaked by this month, mostly because we didn't have to pay for birth control. With all the incentives, it might actually be cheaper to have a baby! I was reading an article about how people with more kids make more money. I think I read if you have three kids you make 7% more, and if you have five kids you make 15% more! One of the guys I work with has seven kids, and he's going to get an award from the company."

Katrina felt panic rise in her chest as he spoke. "Kevin, no. We said no more than two. I never wanted a big family. I thought you were okay with that. You said you were okay with that."

Kevin smiled. "Yeah, I know you didn't want a lot of kids, but maybe this time... it will be a boy." He nudged her a little and waggled his eyebrows, teasing her. But she knew he wasn't teasing.

Katrina scrambled to make a more convincing argument. "Remember how sick I was when I was pregnant with Amy? What if I have another hemorrhage, like with Jessie? I don't want to leave you with two little girls by yourself!"

"That won't happen," Kevin said reassuringly. "Third time's a charm."

Katrina made an exasperated noise, her voice rising. "You're never here, anyway! I feel like I'm barely managing to keep it together now! What are you going to do if I'm gone?"

She could see Kevin wanted to argue, but he held his hands up, surrendering. "Okay, we'll talk about it later. You've got a broken arm! Look, I'm sorry I'm not here much. I'm just trying to take care of us, you know? I miss you like crazy when I'm gone. But I'll tell you what: I'll help out as much as I can with dinner and the girls so you can focus on getting better."

He hugged her, miraculously avoiding jostling her arm. After holding her tightly for a while, he kissed her forehead, then tilted her face up to kiss her eyes, her cheeks, her mouth. It felt good, and it felt good to feel good after the last few weeks. He held her face in his hands and then brought them up the back of her neck through her hair. She shivered.

"Are you trying to get me pregnant again?" she said lightly. Kevin froze, and before she could say anything else, he left the room.

Still, Kevin splurged on pizza for dinner. He was noticeably more relaxed and cheerful. Afterwards, they played a card game with the girls, everyone laughing and talking, napkins and little packets of powdered cheese scattered around the coffee table in the living room. Jessie sang a pop song and Amy tried to sing along with her, the two bouncing and getting the words all wrong. Jessie said she wanted to have pizza every night, and Amy agreed. "Peppawoni!" she yelled.

But a few days later, the smell of scrambled eggs made Katrina gag. She covered the noise by running the water in the bathroom sink until the nausea passed. She splashed her face with cold water and looked at herself in the mirror. Her face was pale and wan, her hazel eyes dull.

She dug beneath the sink to locate the Manual Hormone Detector she had discovered at the bottom of the white paper bag from the clinic. She had hidden it in a box of tampons behind the strawberry-scented bubble bath the girls disliked. Unlike a normal home pregnancy test, the MHD came with a warning label: "For physician use only. Use only in accordance with the American Life Act, Title I, Sec. 1303. Cannot be used to verify paternity or detect fetal defects." But it also wasn't connected to the internet.

Katrina clumsily tore the package open with one hand. She peed on the stick and set it in the sink. She closed her eyes and forced herself to count slowly, listening to the girls clatter and clash as they set the table. When she opened her eyes again, two blue lines stood out clearly against the white porcelain.

Katrina felt dizzy. She braced herself against the sink, taking deep breaths that shook her like sobs. If she had seen two pink lines, it would have been a girl. She couldn't tell Kevin. Not yet.

Amy was trying to open the bathroom door and calling for her. "Okay, baby, wait, I'm coming out," Katrina said. She wrapped the detector in toilet paper and buried it in the trash. With one last breath, she opened the door and both Amy and Jessie piled on her. She kissed Jessie's head and hugged Amy with one arm. Kevin's voice rose from the kitchen: "Be careful with your mommy, girls. Who wants toast?"

•   •   •

When the doorbell rang, Kevin answered the door. Katrina heard some faint murmurings and a nervous laugh. After a few moments, Kevin brought Heather into the dining room. His mouth was thin with resentment and Katrina knew he wanted to stay, but someone had to watch the girls. It wasn't long before she heard Amy shriek with laughter from the living room, and she relaxed a little.

"Hi, Heather," Katrina said. "Thanks for coming."

"Of course," Heather said, a little formally. "It's the right thing to do." She looked uncomfortably away from Katrina's sling. "I'm glad you're all right. I mean, I'm glad it wasn't worse. I mean..."

"It's okay. Have a seat," Katrina said.

"Have you picked up your bike at Jane's yet?" Heather asked, as she perched on the edge of the chair.

"Tomorrow. I have the receipts from the doctor and the physical therapy and the daycare all in here." Katrina tapped on the manila folder on the table.

Heather's face flickered with dismay when she saw the total amount, but they both knew it could have been much worse. Car insurance didn't cover collisions with "non-motorized transport," so people who walked or biked had no protection in accidents. Katrina had been grateful when Heather had promised to pay the bills. But now Heather looked even more miserable than Katrina felt. It both annoyed Katrina and touched her at the same time.

"Don't worry, Heather," Katrina said. "It was just an accident. Everything's going to be all right."

"I told you my sister died, right?" Heather said abruptly, putting her checkbook down. "She fell down the stairs. They said it was an accident. She was pregnant."

Katrina raised her eyebrows. "Oh, no, Heather, that's terrible! I'm so sorry to hear that!"

"But she didn't want the baby. Her fucking husband—sorry—was screwing this woman he met online. He was going to get a divorce. He was going to take the kids. He always said he would. He used to say she was a terrible mom, but then he kept knocking her up. He kept finding excuses to get out of applying for birth control, but he never did a goddamned thing to help out."

Katrina struggled to keep her expression neutral. She had never heard anyone else openly admit to not wanting a child. But when Katrina had learned she was pregnant, she had fantasized about accidents that would be serious enough to cause a miscarriage—but not so serious that she would die and not so obvious that she could be prosecuted for feticide or have her girls taken from her.

Katrina could barely admit to herself that she had begun to ride more quickly than she ordinarily would, taking more chances in traffic. Right before the accident, she had been experimenting with how close she could get to the light rail tracks before her wheels caught in the groove. She would drift close to the tracks and then pull away or weave across the tracks as close to parallel as she could. It had been an almost hypnotic compulsion, and she had been so focused on the tracks she hadn't seen Heather's car as they both entered the intersection.

"I don't think we should be talking about this," Katrina managed to say, unable to look at Heather.

"Yeah, I'm sorry. It's just... she used to rub her stomach like you did when I was taking you home. That's how I figured out she was pregnant. She didn't want to tell me. She lied to me. She said she just had a 'close call' but then after she died it turned out she was pregnant all along. So when you said that, I just freaked out." Heather was on the verge of tears. "I only found out about all this a couple of months ago. I wish I had known sooner. I could have helped her."

Katrina wanted to cry, too. "There's nothing you could have done."

Heather pursed her lips, unconvinced. "I would have taken her to Jane's. They've always been there for me when I needed them. They could have acted as a proxy for her birth control application, at the very least, so she wouldn't have had to depend on her good-for-nothing husband."

Katrina felt like her head was spinning. "Whoah, wait," she said. "I thought you said Jane's was a bike shop?"

"Oh, it is," Heather said. "But it's a collective, so they're also big into community services. If you need something, they'll do everything they can to help you. That's why I wish my sister..." Heather tilted her head back and took a deep, shuddering breath, while Katrina looked on helplessly.

After Heather finally left, Katrina read three stories to Amy and clumsily tucked Jessie into bed. After the last good night, she carefully sat next to Kevin on the couch, leaning against his shoulder. She closed her eyes and took a deep breath, feeling his muscles tense and relax beneath her cheek.

He was watching the news: a national committee was being formed to look into the sharply rising poverty rate. Katrina fumbled for the remote and turned the TV off.

"I don't want to watch this," she said. It was always bad news. Women who hid their pregnancies and then discarded the babies. Parents who killed their daughters and disabled children. Children sold through adoption markets in countries with low birth rates. Little kids dying in industrial accidents. Skyrocketing child abuse, domestic violence, and maternal death rates. And then there were the family suicides. Katrina felt a lump in her throat. She wanted to believe she could never do something so awful.

She pushed those thoughts aside and leaned against Kevin again. "Hey."

Kevin looked down at her. "Hey," he said. Katrina leaned against him harder. Kevin gently pushed back. They continued pushing against each other until they finally kissed. Kissing turned into stroking, Kevin trying to avoid her arm. She pushed harder against him, a little moan escaping her. Kevin slowly stood up. "I haven't applied for birth control yet," he said as he headed towards the guest bedroom and closed the door.

·   ·   ·

The bell rang overhead as Katrina entered Jane's Bicycle Collective. She held Amy's hand as Jessie opened the door wide for all of them.

The shop was comfortable and inviting, with artful colors, good smells, and quiet music. Soft light filtered through plants hanging in the curved windows, accented with colorful paper lanterns. She would even bet the bathroom was clean.

Behind the counter, the bike mechanic was a woman whose silver hair was braided and wrapped around her head. She wore denim overalls and a faded striped shirt. Her wrench flashed as she tightened a bolt on Katrina's bike.

"Hi, how can I help you?" the mechanic asked. Her smile was warm.

"I'm here for that bike," Katrina said, pointing with her chin. She still held Amy's hand.

"You're Katrina?" the mechanic said. "Great, Heather said you'd be in. It's almost ready if you want to take a seat. We've got some stuff for kids, too, if they want." She gestured towards a nearby nook with a couple of cozy purple couches and a plushly upholstered red chair. A selection of periodicals lay on the table. Amy was immediately attracted to a contraption of wires and beads, while Jessie tackled the coloring books and markers set out on a kid-sized table.

Katrina gladly sat down. She was so tired. "Are you Jane?" she asked.

"Oh, no. I'm Maggie. Hi," she said, smiling and waving. "Jane's just what we call the collective."

Maggie gave the bike a last look-over, took it off the stand and wheeled it around the counter. "Well, it's all done! Can I get you some tea?"

"Oh, no, that's OK," Katrina protested.

"You look like you could use a break. It's no trouble."

Katrina softened. Tea might help the nausea. "OK. Uh, something herbal please. I need to avoid caffeine for a while."

After a couple of minutes, Maggie brought them peppermint tea in mismatched mugs. The temperature was just right.

"I heard you had an accident," Maggie said, indicating Katrina's arm. "How are you doing?"

Katrina shrugged with one shoulder. "OK, I guess. Could have been worse."

"How's everything at home?" Maggie asked.

Katrina tried to smile brightly. "Oh, you know, we're getting along. My husband's been really great. The girls have been great, too. We're talking about having my mom fly out here just to have an extra set of hands."

Maggie looked over the rim of the mug kindly. "Well, I'm sorry about the accident, but if you need anything, let us know. We've got a pretty good system to help each other out when stuff like this happens—we can deliver meals, help with household stuff, do physical therapy, child care..." Maggie waved her hand to indicate there was more she couldn't remember, and then: "Oh, we just finished a donation drive for one of our members who had her bike stolen! We could do one for you, too!"

Katrina was impressed. "Oh, wow. Thank you, but I think we're going to be all right."

But things were never going to be all right again. She still hadn't told Kevin she was pregnant. Katrina knew the longer it took her to admit it the harder it was going to be, but every time she thought about it, her brain immediately jumped to another topic. It was as if she was trapped in a haunted house, keeping her eyes shut tight while stumbling in the dark, tense and waiting for the monster to leap out at her. It was all she could think about, and yet she couldn't let herself think about it.

Katrina's face must have given something away. Maggie was looking at her, concerned. Katrina forced a weak smile and started to get up. "Sorry, I'm not feeling well today."

"Oh? What's wrong?"

Katrina shook her head a little and looked around for Jessie and Amy. Jessie was still coloring, while Amy had begun sorting through a bin of bike frame paint samples in the play area. "Just tired," she said.

"You're safe here," Maggie said. "You can talk about it if you want."

Katrina looked at her sharply. But there was no judgment or reservation in Maggie's face, and she waited patiently, mug in her hands, relaxed against the couch. The pause stretched out like a tightrope, and Katrina could feel her heart beat in her ears, fear and hope twisted together in her throat.

"I just... it's been pretty stressful." Katrina ventured, scrutinizing Maggie's reaction. Maggie nodded and waited. "On all of us." Katrina continued, and paused again. She knew Heather trusted Jane's. She remembered the way Paula had risked her job to help her. She let the silence stretch as long as she could, as if waiting for the earth to swallow her whole. When the earth remained still, she took a deep breath. "Even before the accident."

And then everything leaked out of Katrina quietly, slowly. Maggie asked a couple of questions but mostly just let Katrina talk, and when Katrina was done, it was as if she could breathe fully for the first time since she discovered she was pregnant.

"Stop it!" Jessie's voice broke in, trying to keep Amy away from her drawing. And then Amy came to crawl in her lap, and Jessie wanted something to eat, and Katrina realized she still had to go to the grocery store.

So Maggie wheeled the bike to Katrina's car, helped her buckle the girls into their car seats, and put the bike on the bike rack. Before Katrina got into the car, Maggie handed her a red helmet.

"Accidents happen," Maggie said. Her gaze was steady in a way that made Katrina feel both exposed and comforted. "What matters is what you do after an accident. If you need help, go to the address inside this helmet. You're going to be alright."

•   •   •

Katrina clutched the helmet as she walked up to a nondescript office building. Dark mirrored windows distorted her reflection as she approached.

Kevin was back from another trip, so he was watching the girls today as he tried to work from home. She had told him she had another doctor's appointment this afternoon, which wasn't entirely a lie. She hoped Kevin wouldn't notice the withdrawal she made after Heather's check cleared. Lately she felt like she was constantly juggling fire and lies, and she couldn't wait to be done with it.

Inside, a lobby receptionist with an elegant updo turned towards Katrina. There were a few other professional-looking people in the lobby, absorbed by their devices or magazines. Hallways and doors led to unknown business offices. Katrina hadn't expected a place like this, with its tall ceiling and slate tiles. And she certainly hadn't expected anyone else to be here, which made it hard for her to speak the words Maggie had told her to say at the reception desk.

"There's been an accident. I need help," Katrina managed to croak. Her voice echoed in the vast lobby. She had practiced this speech in the bathroom mirror dozens of times, afraid she wouldn't be able to speak the words when the time came, afraid she wouldn't be able to portray a convincing level of pain and fear.

But as she spoke the words, they felt so true that tears immediately welled up and her face curled into itself. The receptionist looked at her kindly and took the helmet.

"They can help you on the fourth floor," she said, motioning towards the elevators. Katrina stepped inside and let the doors slide closed, feeling herself rise.

LIVEWIRE

Ayame Whitfield

"Do bots have consciousness, Dave? It's obvious, in my opinion, that they don't, but there are those among us who ascribe all kinds of emotions and motivations to bots that simply aren't there."

"What do you say to the news that GeoTech Corporation has reportedly produced a line of bots with what they're calling 'emotional processors'?"

"The so-called B15 model? Tch. Foolishness, if you ask me. There's no way you can program feeling into something, no matter how hard you try. It's a facsimile of emotion, that's all."

"To which bots rights activists would say, if there's even the appearance of emotion, we might as well treat them as having emotions."

"Well, Dave, to me that's completely—"

The radio sputtered, swallowing the talk show guest's words in a squeal of digital feedback. Mari pounded the side of the device with a closed fist, scowling darkly.

"Damn stupid thing," she muttered. It was high past time she got a replacement for this old contraption, but she didn't even have the money to pay her cellular bill, let alone for a new radio. She felt like she was trapped in a 21st century home, with her radio and a landlord that shut off her running water whenever her rent was late.

Giving up on resuscitating her radio, she stood up, stretching. Her back cracked as her wrists curled over her head, the sound loud in the silence. Mari lived in one of the valleys of civilization, the lower profile quasi-suburbs stretching between cities that bled together in a land entirely urbanized. There were now only cities of varying sizes, places with buildings tall enough to block out the sky and little to no natural greenery.

She sighed and crossed to the window, peering up at the sliver of sky visible between apartment buildings. Her radio gave a feeble sputter of static and faded into silence.

·   ·   ·

She was biking home from work—no money for the bus, again—when she heard the strange noise coming from an alley near her house. It was soft, nearly lost in the bustle of hovercars passing by overhead, but she heard it nonetheless, a soft clink like metal against stone. She hit the brakes, turning to avoid the omnipresent rubbish of city life, crumpled paper, and bits of plastic caught in the sullen breeze.

In this era of hovercars and elevated walkways, the streets were generally left deserted save for the poor and desperate. (Mari liked to think she fell into the first category only.) It made it dangerous to stay out too long, though.

Mari parked her bike next to the dark mouth of the alley and took one last look around to make sure there weren't any thugs waiting to jump out at her. Looks all clear.

It always looks clear until they jump you, a snide voice in the back of her mind pointed out. Mari ignored it. Sometimes, valuable things ended up in the trash, despite the city's disposal ordinances. Maybe this would be her big break, finding some hidden cache of money in a rusty old dumpster.

She approached the metal container, trying to walk as softly as she could. Here and there, the sidewalk was still spotted with black relics of chewing gum mingled with spilled oil from the hovercraft that buzzed by overhead. Moss grew in the alleyway, splotches of green scattered like puddles of plant life on the broken concrete. Lichen and moss and algae were about the only things that thrived in this world anymore when it came to plant life.

There was a foot sticking out of the rubbish beside the dumpster.

Mari regarded it, more curious than afraid. It was plastic, with a sheen to it that suggested newness. There was a scar on the sole, as if it had tread on something sharp, marring the smooth surface. A black tarp was thrown over it as if to hide whatever was under it.

She cautiously lifted the corner of the tarp, revealing the leg that the foot was connected to. It was the same plastic, pale skin tone shining in the dim light of the alley.

She ripped the tarp aside.

A body lay propped against the building, eyes closed. It had no hair, and given that it was also naked, Mari could see enough to deduce that it was modeled after a female human. Its limbs were jointed cunningly so that she could barely see where the plastic joined to plastic, but it was clearly artificial.

Two things occurred to her at once.

One: this was clearly a bot.

Two: unregistered, working bots fetched thousands of dollars on the black market, maybe more than Mari made in a year at her clerk job.

She hadn't paid much attention in her Home Ec high school classes, but she knew enough to poke at power switches and do some basic cross-wiring. How hard could it be to get this bot awake again?

Mari bent down and lifted the bot's arm. The smooth surface felt strange against her fingers. She searched for a power button, found one on the back of its neck. Holding her breath, hardly daring to hope, she pressed it.

A blue light flickered to life in the bot's eyes, a soft whirring under its skin that Mari could feel against her fingers. After a moment, the bot sat up and looked at her.

Mari swallowed. "Hi."

"Hello." The bot's voice was smooth and female.

"Do you have a—" She had almost said name. As if a bot could have a name. "A serial number?"

"R2947327," the bot replied promptly.

"R two nine—you know, I'll just call you R. You okay with that?" A beat of silence. "Of course you are. Silly me."

R regarded her. "And what shall I address you as?"

"Um. I'm Mari."

"Ms. Mari." R folded in on herself, then stood. She was several inches taller than Mari, who found herself craning her neck to maintain eye contact.

"Just Mari is fine. Let's get you into my apartment, shall we?"

·   ·   ·

She found an old blouse and skirt for it to wear in the back of her closet. Intellectually, she knew it didn't matter if it was unclothed, because it wasn't really human, but she still felt more comfortable when it had clothes on.

"Stay put," she ordered it the next morning, wheeling her bike to the door as she prepared to head out for work. "If anyone finds out you're here, it won't be good. Try to be quiet."

R nodded. "I shall be quiet."

"Good." Mari hesitated. The silence that filled the room was awkward, but she felt like there was something else she should say. Before she could, R spoke again.

"Mari?"

"Yes?"

"Be safe." There was something strangely like feeling in the bot's voice.

Mari frowned. "I—okay?"

As suddenly as the feeling had appeared, R's tone faded back to cool detachment. "See you later."

●　　　●　　　●

Mari swung by the plant depot on her way home to pick up a new set of windowsill plants. They were part of her quota of oxygen-producing life, along with the communal algae tank at the top of the building, and crowned her window with green, the light filtering through the leaves and casting dappled shadows on the floor. She was awful at keeping them alive, hence the monthly trips to the depot.

When she got home, she paused in front of her door, pressing her ear to the cold metal to see if she could hear anything suspicious going on inside. It wasn't that she thought R was up to anything, it was just—she wanted to be sure to catch it in the act if it was doing something strange. There were no noises from inside, and she did not want to linger too long in the hallway (it would be hard to explain why she was standing outside her own apartment with her ear against the door), so she inserted her keycard into the lock and pushed the door open.

R was sitting in the center of the living room, surrounded by feathers.

"What the hell?" Mari snapped, closing the door sharply behind her. It looked up, blue flashing in its eyes.

"Mari. You are home."

"What did you—did you take apart a pillow?" Mari bent down, picked up a handful of feathers. "Why on earth would you do that?"

"Are they real, Mari?"

"Of course not. You think I'd be living here if I could afford real down pillows?" She dropped the feathers, disgusted. "You made a mess. Clean it up."

"I am not a service bot."

Mari stared. "Did you honestly just talk back to me? Clean it up or I'll turn you in."

"You would not be doing the turning in." There was a hint of purple flooding the blue of R's digital eyes. "If they find me, they'll fine you five thousand dollars."

"Five thousand—" Mari felt suddenly unsteady on her feet. "I don't make that much in six months."

R's lips lifted in a facsimile of a smile, its only response.

Mari groaned and went to find a broom.

· · ·

R powered down for the night, and Mari watched it as it lay motionless, standby light flickering erratically. It was strange, she thought, to have a bot in her house. It filled the room with a soft, almost imperceptible hum, like electricity crackling along the hairs on her arm.

A half-formed thought had been niggling the back of her mind all day.

It acts so human.

It was a strange thought to have when it was so clearly artificial. But R was a strange bot. In Mari's (limited) experience, bots were supposed to be servile. They were programmed, inherently, to serve. Even if the more advanced models had bio-generated flesh and blood, even if they looked human, they were composed at their very core of electricity and wires and little ones and zeroes in infinite strings. They weren't supposed to express emotion beyond what they were programmed to do—like pleasure bots, faking happiness and flirtation and all the other things people wanted to pay for. Just because it looked like they had feelings didn't mean they did.

But there was something about R that gave her pause. Maybe it was just that she had not spent much time around bots because her parents had been poor and she was poor now, but R felt strangely—almost—human.

Not like a complete human, though. Mari had spent some time around children and it was strange how similar looking after R felt. Almost as if the bot was just a child, exploring this new world, reaching out to grasp at a humanity that felt like her birthright.

She would never be human, but that didn't mean she wasn't acting human.

Maybe the bots rights activists were right. Maybe that was all that mattered.

·   ·   ·

"It's twelve noon and time for the top of the hour news report. Police say they have apprehended the man who destroyed B15-T, the first known bot with a so-called 'emotional processor'. Bots rights activist Elizabeth Tyler is here to discuss the situation. Elizabeth, what do you have to say about this?"

"This arrest is the first step in the right direction, Dave. The next would be to prosecute the criminal not as a destroyer of property, but as a murderer."

"Don't you think that's a bit extreme?"

"Far from it. B15-T was a feeling, thinking being. If ending his life was not murder, then neither is killing a human."

.   .   .

"Where did you come from?" she asked R. The bot had been staying in her apartment for about a week at that point, long enough that it was beginning to feel like a permanent fixture. Mari still hadn't gotten around to figuring out who she could contact in the black market, but as soon as she did, R was gone.

Or at least that was what she kept telling herself. The truth was, she had gotten used to seeing R around and might even miss it when it was gone.

"An Exgen plant. I am part of their fifth line of interpretation bots."

"So you must know a lot of languages," Mari mused.

"Two thousand and seventy."

Mari's eyes widened. I didn't know there were that many languages in the world, she almost said, but feared it would make her sound uncultured and ignorant. "How did you end up in a trashcan in my alley?"

R considered this for a moment, blue eyes darkening slightly. "I do not remember."

"That must be difficult for you," Mari said without thinking. R's lips turned down in a frown.

"How so?"

"I mean, you're a bot." She winced at the obvious statement but forged onwards. "You're built to be infallible. So if you can't remember something that happened to you, it means you've failed."

"Or that my programming was at fault."

"So you don't blame yourself."

"Why would I? I do not recall doing anything wrong. Would you blame yourself, if you suffered from amnesia?"

Mari laughed. "Fair enough."

·　　　·　　　·

It was only later that night, when Mari was in bed, that she realized how easy it was becoming to interact with R. Words that came awkwardly around others flowed freely with her. R was attentive, and she responded intelligently. It felt like talking to an old friend.

Or you're just lonely and desperate for anyone to talk to.

She rolled over, pulling her blankets tighter around herself. Across the room, R's internal fans whirred. Lulled by the noise, Mari drifted off to sleep.

·　　　·　　　·

"Reports are coming in all over the city of what bots rights activists are terming hate crimes committed against bots, perpetrated by people emboldened by the recent destruction of B15-T. Police say there is rampant destruction of property across the borough but refuse to say what, if anything, they will do about it. Those apprehended have cited fears that bots are becoming too human and must be reprogrammed before they become smarter than us. Several instances of breaking and entering have occurred..."

·　　　·　　　·

Mari had never biked home faster.

It was only concern for her investment, she told herself, pedaling furiously down the street. She took a sharp left to avoid a pothole and nearly toppled over. The fact that her heart had nearly stopped at the holovision report that people were breaking into houses to forcibly reprogram bots meant nothing. It wasn't as if she was worried about R and her wellbeing.

What if someone found her?

She reached her apartment building and pedaled straight through the lobby, screeching to a halt in front of the elevator. Hammering the button to summon it, she shifted from foot to foot, impatient. When it finally came, she pushed her bike in. It rose painfully slowly, numbers ticking by—two, three, four.

The elevator deposited her on the fifth floor, and Mari tore down the hallway, dropping her bike and fumbling for her keycard.

She wrenched opened the door.

R stood in the sunlight, shadows from the plants on the windowsill dappling the pale plastic of her arms. In the light, the bot seemed gilded. Something strange and warm swelled in Mari's heart, rising in her throat and choking her. At the sound of the door, R turned towards her. She regarded Mari for a moment, then tilted her head to one side.

"You look worried."

Mari crossed the room in two strides and kissed her. R's lips were smooth and cold, plastic hardly even warming against her skin even when R parted her lips, letting Mari slip her tongue into the strange depths of her mouth.

She's safe, Mari thought, and felt her entire body relax.

"I am not programmed as a pleasure bot," R told her when they pulled apart. "Nor am I programmed to feel love."

"I can live with that." Mari reached up, ran a hand down R's cheek, her skin shockingly dark against the nearly white plastic. "May I?"

R nodded. She pressed another kiss to the bot's lips and almost imagined she felt R responding in turn.

·   ·   ·

It was only because she was so lonely, she told herself. She wasn't in love with a bot. That would be ridiculous. It had just been so long since she had had—physical companionship. She had no feelings towards R except those appropriate to feel towards a bot.

And she would keep reminding herself of that as much as she had to, she concluded, snuggling further into R's embrace. The bot's arms had warmed to her skin, and Mari was starting to get used to the feeling of plastic against her. It felt nice to simply exist with someone else, warm and safe, even if it was an illusion.

·   ·   ·

"What do you think of this?" Mari gestured at the radio on the table between them, where reports were crackling in about protests, demonstrations, people marching in the streets with signs like equal rights for all and bots have souls too and justice for B15-T.

"It is foolish." R tilted her head to one side, bird-like. "Why, what do you think?"

"I mean, if he had emotions—"

"It did not. Believe me."

Mari frowned. "How would you know?"

R regarded her coldly, eyes a flat blue. "I am a bot. We understand our own kind. Bots do not have emotions, nor do they have true consciousness. Therefore we cannot be murdered."

"Or do you only think that because you've been programmed to?"

"Do you think I am conscious?"

"Yes!" Mari clenched her fists. "You're talking to me about yourself, you know you're alive, you kissed me back—"

"You deceive yourself." R's face, so meticulously crafted, stubbornly showed no expression at all. Mari wanted her to be angry, to shout back. "I am not alive, and I certainly did not kiss you back."

"That's what they want you to think."

"If you wish to continue to spout forth these conspiracy theories, feel free to." R stood, pushing her chair away from the table. "I will be in the back room."

"You mean my room." Mari stood, as well, glaring. "You're in my house, and I could turn you in if I wanted. Say you wandered in and I went to the police immediately."

R paused. "I would inform them of the truth."

"Who would believe you?" Mari scoffed. "You're a bot. They'd reprogram you, or you'd end up on some scrap heap in their factories."

A strange spasm crossed R's face and she turned away. When she spoke, her voice sounded strangled. "Do not turn me in, Mari. Please."

Mari's mouth shut with a click. Just as quickly as it had come, the expression on R's face faded away. Shocked, she watched R disappear into the back room.

·   ·   ·

On her way home from work, she stopped by a public library to use one of the computer terminals, hitching her bike to a streetlamp before scurrying up the stairs into the cool, dark confines of the library. Hardly anyone was there, so it was easy to secure a terminal.

What does an emotional processor look like? she typed into the search bar, then navigated to images. Committed them to memory rather than printing them out, since she didn't have enough money on her card to afford the paper, and biked back home, wondering.

· · ·

Mari woke at two in the morning exactly, hand flying to her alarm clock to silence it. She paused, waiting. The blue glow from the other side of the room did not brighten—R was still asleep. This was the best chance she was going to get.

She slipped out of bed and padded over to where R sat. Hesitating for a split second, she reached up and pressed R's power button. Her standby light powered down. Feeling slightly guilty, Mari flipped open the panel on the back of R's smooth head, leaning in close to examine the interior by the orange light from the streetlight outside.

· · ·

The next morning, R approached her. "You turned me off last night. May I ask why?"

Mari pointed at her accusingly. "You're one of the B15 models. You lied to me."

R regarded her calmly. "I did."

"Bots aren't supposed to be able to do that."

"We can," she said simply.

"Because you were programmed to?"

"No. It is an unintended side effect of the emotional processor, one that GeoTech intended to be eradicated in the next model."

"B15-T?"

"Yes."

"So how come you ended up in my alley? Did you run away?"

R nodded.

"Why?"

The bot raised one eyebrow. "Why do you think?"

Mari hesitated, then her eyes widened. "You were afraid. Afraid of dying, weren't you."

"I was. I still am."

"So you do feel things. I was right."

R shrugged. "I do not know if I feel things as humans do."

Mari shook her head, still trying to process this. Finding R in the alley had felt no different from finding some other valuable object, but in truth, R had been a refugee among the city skyscrapers. It had been so easy to treat R like a thing, but she had had emotions the entire time.

"None of us know," she said at length. "We're only stuck in our own heads, experiencing our own feelings. Maybe none of us feel things the same way. Doesn't make your feelings—or mine—any less valid."

"I had not thought of it that way." R looked thoughtful. "Regardless. What will you do with me now that you know?"

"I don't see how this changes our situation." She watched R relax slightly, tension flowing out of her shoulders. "Except—"

"Yes?"

"I don't want to do anything to you that you don't want. So don't hide your feelings from me anymore." Mari smiled at her, and watched as R hesitated, then smiled back.

"I won't."

. . .

It might be unsustainable, keeping an unregistered bot in her apartment, Mari thought—especially a bot that GeoTech was likely looking high and low for—but something about R made it worth it.

They slept in the same bed, now, warm limbs tangled with plastic. Sometimes, R would twitch in her sleep, powered down eyes flickering with a faint light. Mari wondered if the emotional processor allowed her to dream.

Well. She could ask her tomorrow.

Smiling, Mari curled up next to R, wrapping an arm around her and closing her eyes.

THERE WERE ONE AND MANY

Kat Lerner

I didn't know what to expect when I decided to come to Earth. But if you had told me that a month later I would be escaping my host family's residence on a manually-driven single-track vehicle, I might have reconsidered.

Growing up a half-human on Noeria IV, traveling to Earth had been my lifelong dream. I never met my human parent, but when other Noerians looked at me, I felt like my alienness—my humanity—was all they saw. On Earth, I thought, among humans, things would be different. Well, I wasn't wrong.

The host family I was assigned to consisted of four humans: Morty, a tall parent with a bald spot like one of the Xnoths' old crop circles; Barb, a short parent who enjoyed consuming large amounts of an alcoholic compound called gin; and two offspring, Trent and Suzy, who were always off riding horses in funny clothes.

They picked me up right from the spaceport tarmac, holding a sign reading my name, "Ji Aui'a" surrounded by characters with green, balloon-shaped heads.

That must be their favorite cartoon, I thought as I climbed in their hovercar. I don't know many cartoons. What if I don't have anything to talk to them about?

Thankfully, Morty just chattered about other planets he had visited, intermittently turning to Barb to emphasize "on business." Barb seemed not to hear and continued spraying a harsh-smelling liquid on every surface I touched.

When we drove into their neighborhood, Ivory Heights, and Morty finally lowered the blackout curtains on the hovercar windows, I pressed my face to the glass to take in my first real look at Earth. But instead of the sky-high neon buildings I'd seen in those few bootlegged Earth shows, I saw rows of identical houses—ranch style in mint green, lemon chiffon yellow, and flamingo pink, as Barb named them, the pattern repeating until I lost my sense of how far we'd traveled.

Morty and Barb lived in a mint green house in the middle of one of these roads.

"Honestly, I didn't know how you would be able to find your house among so many identical structures, especially since we've been driving through Ivory Heights for almost an hour," I said cheerfully, "but I see you could tell by how many more hovercars you own compared to your neighbors." I nodded at the shiny silver crafts littering their driveway and curb and wondered what they did with all of them.

Barb inhaled sharper than necessary through her nose and breezed towards the front door. "We're throwing a welcome party for you. We invited all of Section Q4."

"Thank you!" I said, my bioluminescent patterns glowing warmly.

Despite the warning, when Morty opened the door, I jumped. Across the threshold stood a crowd of middle-aged humans wearing giant almond-shaped sunglasses, floppy aluminum antennae, and chains of artificial flowers.

"It's a Luau on Mars theme!" Barb cried as a short human bedecked me with two flower chains and antennae attached to a headband. "We thought it'd make you feel more at home."

"Oh no." My lights flared. "Were you expecting an exchange from Mars?"

"It's the same climate, right?" Morty said, resting a hand on Barb's shoulder.

"Errr…"

"Enough talking. Why don't you go mingle?" Barb said, pushing me through the front door and walking off. "Who's up for martinis?"

Left alone with the crowd of brightly clad humans, I tried to imagine what "mingle" could entail besides talking. The other humans, however, clearly did not care about Barb's directive as they circled closer around me.

"So what do we call you?" one large human asked.

"Ji Aui'a," I said, my voice cracking. I cleared it. "It means 'one who sees the path.'"

"Hmm, let's call you Dana, okay? Now Dana, tell us everything about yourself."

I took a deep breath. I had been expecting many questions about Noeria, and now I figured it would be beneficial considering their apparent lack of access to elementary-level astronomy. But before I could answer, a taller human in loose shorts and a shirt displaying tropical scenery walked up to the group and gestured toward me with a plastic beverage container in the shape of a coconut.

"Is it a he or a she, then?"

I blinked. "I am a Noerian."

"Yes, I was wondering that, too," a short, yellow-haired human said, not seeming to hear me. "You look a little soft to be a boy, and your cheekbones are quite feminine."

"You're blind as a bat, Margaret," another said, turning my face sideways. "When have you seen such masculine ears on a girl?"

"Your mother actually," Margaret replied, yanking my earlobe. I inched backwards.

"The Noerians do not categorize—"

"Oh, come now, don't try to give us that alien nonsense. They said you were half-human, right?" the one in the tropical shirt said, turning to the others. "I mean, how will I know whether to be embarrassed if it sees me naked?"

Margaret's eyes narrowed.

A similar-looking tall human leaned in. "We keep telling you, Bill. There's no reason to take your pants off after golf. Just wear your khakis home."

Suddenly, Morty and Barb appeared behind me.

"We're thinking boy," Barb said, and Morty nodded.

"He's a little scrawny right now, but I'm sure he'll grow into a strapping young man soon." Morty slapped my back, almost pitching me into the humans' colorful beverages.

"Or who knows?" Margaret said. "Maybe your men just look like women."

"Better watch your boy Trent that he doesn't catch anything," Bill drawled.

The crowd laughed.

"I was fully immunized before departure from Noeria IV," I stated, trying not to feel offended.

The laughter faltered and died.

"Why don't you go see your room?" Barb suggested, guiding me by the shoulders towards the stairs.

I climbed them slowly, listening to the chatter below picking up again.

"You know," one high voice began, "we had a gardener once who was an alien."

A lower voice was quick to answer. "Helen, I told you, he was from Canada."

I wasn't sorry to leave the scene. Tomorrow was another day, I reminded myself, with a whole new world to see.

·   ·   ·

I was glad my host family gave me a bicycle instead of a hovercar like Trent and Suzy had. Hovercars were cramped and smelled of synthetic chemicals. I loved the feeling of the breeze whipping around me on a bicycle, and after only three weeks of constant practice and fourteen superficial wounds, I'd finally learned to ride it without falling over.

Gliding over the smooth street, I counted the flamingo pink houses (my favorites, though I wouldn't tell Barb and Morty that). Sometimes, next to a hovercar, I would see a man hunched over, leisurely rubbing the metal surface. I knew they were men now. Barb had explained that only men polished their hovercars, so that was one way to tell. I was still working out how to know otherwise, since humans seemed to get offended if you asked. There were just so many exceptions to every rule. Morty told me, "The long-haired ones are girls," but when we went to a movie, and I asked to confirm that the main actor—a human with bulging muscles and long, flowing golden hair—was a woman, Barb pretended not to hear me for the rest of the film.

"Why don't they just tattoo it on their foreheads?" I muttered, swinging my foot out and kicking a rare pebble.

I knew I wasn't really frustrated about not understanding a human custom. I didn't understand football either, and I wasn't losing sleep over it. I was frustrated because I thought things would be different for me here. They were too different and not different enough.

And a little voice in my head kept whispering, "If not here, then where?"

I forced it down and kept riding, until the sun disappeared into the horizon and a sliver of the Earth's moon was illuminated in the sky. I looked to the mint green house on my left, half-expecting to see Morty's hovercar.

But I was somewhere new.

This street ended in a cul-de-sac, the end house framed by a wall of poplars. I looked over my shoulder and then back around, trying to see past the tree trunks. Hopping off my bicycle, I walked it between the houses, under the rustling leaves, and gasped. A sloping field opened up before me. Manicured green lawn gave way to long grasses rippling in the wind like water. Trees dotted the field in the distance, and the moon cast everything in a pale silver glow.

"How far could it be to the neon buildings?" I wondered aloud. Images of the Earth I had dreamed about danced in my mind. Canyons. Vending machines. People wearing cowboy hats. Monuments that served no purpose but to be seen, and structures built just to prove they could be.

A car horn snapped me back to my senses, and I turned to look down the tidy suburban street. I felt a thread of guilt tug at my chest. My host family had taken me in, asking nothing of me but to assimilate into their ways, and I hadn't even been able to do that. My alienness seemed to embarrass them in front of others, but as Morty explained, I looked too human for it to be entertaining. They deserved better, I decided.

I yanked the old cell phone Morty and Barb had given me from my pocket and typed: Thank you for everything. I'm leaving now. I will return with a gender. I considered for a second and sent another: :) Nodding to myself, I grabbed the handlebars and pushed off onto the field.

•   •   •

Everything I learned next confused me more, but at least the food was better.

No offence to Barb's meatloaf and peas, but they just couldn't compare to fluffy pancakes from Sal's Greasy Bucket diner or bear claws and jars of honey from the Western Cryptid Museum gift shop. I learned seventeen unique uses for the Earth potato and what a Kohlrabi was.

I still hadn't found a gender I liked, but I was sure I was making progress.

I learned it was better not to tell people my mission directly, as their responses tended to fall into either "strange look and swift exit" or "knowing look and bad advice." Instead, I asked people about themselves. What clothes did they like to wear? What did they do for fun? What was their opinion on seasonal hot beverages? Humans seemed to love sharing their opinions, and each had an opinion, a taste, a preference, on virtually every subject. The only thing humans seemed to love more than talking about themselves was helping someone become just like them.

In a dusty town with only four buildings, a man who called himself The Conch Cowboy bought me boots with seashells on the tops. He called me John.

Above a Chinese restaurant in a city full of sweet-smelling smoke, a woman who called herself Psychic Sandra taught me to make a voodoo doll. I made one of myself because I wanted to try acupuncture. She called me Zhalana.

On a park bench, an old woman with centimeter-thick glasses called me her daughter, Rose.

In a building made of glass and steel, men in blue suits and identical haircuts taught me about tax cuts. They kicked me out.

•   •   •

Riding through a red desert under a purple twilight, I felt my nerves fraying. Why were humans so hard to understand? They all wanted me to be like them but were so stubbornly against being like other people. Men and women came in so many different variations, the words didn't seem to have much meaning. I wondered if I should just pick one and forget about it.

I wondered if I should have tried harder to fit in on Noeria.

Just then, as if the Earth could hear me thinking of my home planet, my bicycle jerked. I had run over something sharp. I could see it sticking from my front tire, slapping against the asphalt and grinding me to a halt.

I stood still, staring down at the deflated tire as moments ticked by. Finally sliding off, I parked it, sat by a cluster of rocks eerily reminiscent of human phalluses, and sighed.

"This was a bad idea," I said, looking up at the stars twinkling to life above me. "I was a bad idea, wasn't I? Creating me with a human. There are no other Noerian-human hybrids." I looked down at my jeans, already covered in red dust. "Maybe we weren't meant to be combined."

I sat there until the first birds began singing into the dark night, eager for dawn. I thought I was starting to hallucinate when I saw the glowing forms moving toward me. I scrunched my eyes, unable to clear the vision—dark beings covered in neon patterns like my own bioluminescent network.

"Did...did the Noerian Guard come to rescue me?" The fact that I had only been broken down for four hours escaped me as I stumbled out into the road and waved my arms. "I'm here!" I called in Noerian. "My bicycle is broken!"

"Sorry?" one replied in English as they stopped before me. It was a human. At least thirty humans. On bikes.

"I thought you were Noerians," was all I could manage.

"Noeria IV? In the Nephelia System?" another asked.

"Heck, far as I been is New Jersey."

"I've been there," came a soft voice. A young human stepped forward, covered in loopy patterns and long hair haloed in moonlight.

"To New Jersey?" I said dumbly.

The young human grinned. "No, to Noeria. You probably thought we were from there because of the glowing, right? It's just paint to keep us from running into each other."

"Oh," I said, unsure of what else to say.

After a few beats of silence, the young human spoke again. "You said your bike was busted?"

"Yikes, that's a nasty hunka glass you've got in there," another confirmed before I could reply. "Who has the patchin' kit?"

"I do," the young human said, grabbing a backpack and squatting next to my bike.

"It'll have to hold until we can get it replaced, Bee," one on the far side called, "so do a really good job."

"Thanks for the advice," Bee said dryly. "By the way, what's your name?"

I hesitated. "Ji Aui'a."

"Nice to meet ya, Ji Aui'a." Bee looked up from the patches and glue, meeting me with kind eyes. I felt like I was speeding down a hill.

As Bee worked, an elder with bright purple hair under a rainbow helmet shimmied through the pack. "So what're you doing out here, if you don't mind me askin'?"

I wasn't sure if "here" meant this particular road, the desert, or Earth in general, but for some reason, I felt like telling them everything.

They nodded along as I spoke, humming every so often to emphasize their agreement. When I finished, the purple-haired elder waddled forward and laid a hand on my shoulder. "You know, I've traveled the cosmos, too, and after looking into faces of every shape, size, and color, still the only one that matches me 100% is my own reflection, and I make pretty lousy company sometimes."

"It's true," said an elder with a gray beard.

The purple-haired human shot the other an unimpressed look and turned back to me. "Look, honey. You don't need to match anyone 100%."

"Maxine's right," Bee said, standing up and giving my wheel a spin. "Just stick with people who let you be and don't ask a lot of nosy questions."

"Yeah, and if you can't find any, try lizards. They don't judge." Maxine wagged a bony finger.

"Oh," I said again. "Well, would it be nosy to ask…if you are 'he' or 'she'?"

"They," Bee smiled, stepping back toward the pack. "Anyway, ride with us until you get that tire replaced. We know a repair shop in the next town."

"It's next to the Belgian waffles place!" came a voice from the rear of the pack.

"Then ride with us until waffles." Bee laughed, looking over at me. "That work for you?"

Feeling like I was in zero gravity, I nodded. "That works for me."

THE TOWER

Elly Blue

It's almost too cold to ride this morning. I stand, doing my deep breathing and shuffling my feet with small, alternating stomps as Clara wheels the bike out of the shed, pumps two pounds of air into each tire, and checks the brakes, hubs, cables, pedals. There's never an issue, but she does it with thorough yet quick attention, her breath pooling around her in the frosty air. Even when she stands and hands the bike to me, she avoids my eyes, all according to protocol. If I succeed in my training, I will never again make eye contact with another human. An especially hard shiver rocks me.

It's precisely 4:45 when I grasp the handlebars, throw my leg over the back, and push off. I keep a steady clip of 18 miles per hour according to the dinky handlebar speedometer. The extra effort going up the slight slope, the winding of the electric fence next to me, the constant slight attention of dodging larger rocks in the dirt track as I go — it's all as automatic to me as breathing now, or the rest of my daily routine of study and exercise back in the tower. These morning bicycle workouts are the one time of the day I can let my mind be free. Sometimes, I just let it roam over the fields, noting the grazing cows, the clouds, the temperature, the inner workings of my body and breath. Other days, I live out past scenarios—happy or shameful, wondering or infuriated—or future ones, fuzzily imagined snippets of my life in the stars. Today, it's so cold my mind retreats into the smallest part of itself, its clockwork moving so subtly my conscious self can barely grasp it. The bulk of my attention is on simply moving so that the organism that is my body can stay warm enough to continue living.

Which is why I don't notice the obstacle in the road until the bike comes to an abrupt halt, flinging me over the handlebars. Dazed, I jump to my feet, reflexively aware of the need to keep moving. And, more important, the need to be okay, unharmed, and back on schedule so there is no appearance of incident or wavering from my goal. I begin to mentally and visually check each part of me—fingers, hands, forearms, elbows. As I turn my head to check my left shoulder, I catch the dark shape in the corner of my eye, which interrupts my protocol. My bike is sprawled caddywompus in the road, and under it a crumpled form that—yes, it's a human shape. Not moving. I walk towards it, a hard core forming in my stomach and rising to my throat.

The figure is oddly familiar, and then I realize—she is wearing my clothes, she has my build and height. I check under the hats and balaclavas and mask for a pulse that isn't there and see pale skin, a wisp of blonde hair. She's not me, I think to myself, almost say out loud. I look around for a bicycle, and there it is, off to the side. Not exactly the same as mine— all of our equipment is old and cobbled together, for all it's expertly maintained. Another starpilot candidate. What mishap led her here?

I'm frozen with fear and quickly realize I'm also freezing with cold. I pick up my bike. The handlebars are askew by a centimeter but it can't be helped. For a moment, indecision: Do I go back or continue my routine? I can't feel my left foot and realize I have no time left to choose. I throw my leg woodenly over the bike and pedal forward, because it's the only direction I've known for the past 216 days.

I ride, keeping to an average of 22 mph despite, and because of, the growing pain in my left toes, the sharp pins of the air in my lungs. The pace required to get back to the tower on time is an easy mental equation, almost restful compared to the interstellar trajectory problems I will spend the next 3 hours tackling after my return, following a quick high-protein, complex-mineral-infused breakfast mush. I feel a rush of glory, subsuming even the pain of my warming, working body. My mind is sharp, my self-control is unparalleled. I am the future hope of my generation and I will overcome all obstacles to pilot them to the stars, even...

Even. A chemical jolt rushes through me. I've had enough psych training, 216 hours worth, every evening after post-dinner skills review and before my 45 minutes of body care and 30 of reading a literary story before a drug-aided sleep. I know exactly what I've been doing: denying is an approved method of short term coping with a deeply disturbing or damaging event, and my denial has just worn off. I breathe deeper, as I've practiced many times, feeling each movement of breath, turning my awareness to every part of my body. I look down and see that I've dropped to 17 mph and pick up the pace. Based on where I am, and the time, ramping up to 24 mph should catch me up. I will my attention to the road ahead, dodging the rocks, making it a game. I'll think about this while I eat, I promise myself. I'm not supposed to—I have 12 minutes to eat my mush and have been trained to practice mindfulness for better digestion. But there's been a rupture in the order of my day and I need to set my brain to rights before I can sit still for three hours, with perfect, luminous focus and solve for encountering an unexpected comet. I've seen plenty of dead people before. There's always shock, but it never lasts long.

Under the level of my expertly focused attention, my brain is still processing everything: the fall, the body, the break in protocol. And more: another tower, across the plains, as isolated as mine. An attendant, like Clara. Cameras. Mush. Math. I imagine her genius, her determination, a match for mine, and her life—what hardship led her to this isolated existence? Whatever it was, it was certainly not encoded in her skin, and at this my thoughts harden. It's a shame, but she was my rival. And she has not been through what I have, in the schools and on the streets in the wreckage of this white nation. Only the best three of dozens will pilot the colony ships to the stars. She didn't make the cut. I will.

I pedal on, warming, resolved. But I know, in my analytical heart, that I won't report what I saw. It can only reflect badly on my psych evaluation.

Back at the tower, Clara takes my bike and mask and checks my vitals, frowning. "Your heart rate is too elevated," she says, glancing briefly, sidelong, toward my face. I had developed a careful plan to blame a rock, a momentary lapse of attention, the extreme cold. But instead, in the painful heat of the entrance shed that is kept at just above freezing, I find that I'm sobbing. She frowns.

"It's too cold out there," she says. "You'll need an extra eight minutes to warm up before it's safe to return to room temperature." Still looking away, she holds my thickly gloved hand in hers in silence as I weep.

Indoors, under the scrutiny of the cameras that are my constant companions, I chew my mush slowly and let the knots in my mind start to loosen. My skin feels like delicate paper, my eyes and throat thick. While I cried in the shed, the pressure of Clara's mitten on my mitten, all I could think about was my great-grandmother, the civil rights advocate. I never met her, but my parents' house was full of photos of her and everything anyone in my family did was in her name or her honor. My brother rebelled, or rather cracked under the pressure. I embraced her legacy twice as hard. I would be the first, the best, the most whole, the savior of myself, my family, and humanity. When I was accepted into the starpilot training program, it was like all the generations before me had lifted me, had lifted our family, lifted humanity.

The inhumanity of the training program was its appeal. The automation, discipline, isolation, the prospect of being pushed physically and mentally to the very limits of what a person was capable of, all stoked something deep in me. I was born for this, made for this. My great-grandmother had been shaped for equivalent glory, but ahead of her time. I could live it for her.

But in reality, I think now, I'm human too. Pushing the limits of that human capability has made me hyper aware of my fragility, a soft animal with a flawed mind and vulnerable heart. As I swallow the familiar slimy blandness, it sticks in my throat and I cough several times before Clara hands me a glass of water. I think about Clara, who typically blends into the sameness of my days, and wonder what motivates her. I think about the other candidate—what killed her? Did she hit a rock, blinded by the cold as I was? And land badly, hit her head? Did her system just fail from cold and exertion and long months of training? An undetected aneurysm or heart defect?

Or did someone stop her?

I take another bite, steadier than I've ever been, a cool calm of dissociation washing over me. My thoughts are like pebbles falling into a clear lake one at a time. I know I have to snap myself out of it, so I do, looking at a spot on the ceiling, then at my spoon, then setting it down and standing, stretching my arms up over my head to pop my shoulders, the left one, I notice, a little stiff from my fall. Clara whisks the bowl away, and I'm equal parts annoyed and comforted by her sudden visibility.

I get up from the breakfast table and climb the ladder up to my work room, bare except for its broad, tilted desk, eight minutes behind schedule to the second. A view of the empty plain stretches out before me. I dutifully turn to the drill packet on the table. It is not the promised meteor drill, but rather an alternate lift-off calculation for an early spring departure. Strange. But there is no time to ask questions—there's a starship to launch and planets to dodge! Today, the computer is still shut away; my calculations are to be done manually first. I pick up the first in my row of sharpened pencils, open the booklet to the first page, and lose myself in the numbers.

The next morning, my body hurts and I find I fiercely, deeply, don't want to go out on the bicycle. But I do anyway, out of habit and muscle memory and sheer determination. That was yesterday, this is today, I tell myself. Today, it's not quite as bitterly cold. Something has shifted in my mind, and it won't get comfortable, even once we pass the place where the body had been. Instead, I watch my thoughts whirr, moan, and roar, circling tightly back on themselves.

What if someone stopped her?

An absurd thought because who? And why? We're as guarded as we are isolated out here on the plains, our every moment and movement monitored, no chance of encountering even each other, much less a hostile stranger. If our keepers wanted to do one of us in, they'd simply put something lethal in her nightly sleep shot. No drama, no fuss, no messy bodies being found in the road by other candidates. She fell off her bike and hit her head, I convince myself. They hadn't yet noticed or responded to her failure to return to her tower on time. She must have been near the farthest point of her trip. It's not only a perfectly logical explanation, it's the only one.

As I sail through the one crossroads on my route, I habitually, pointlessly look left and right for the cross traffic that will never arrive. But then again my mind continues disobediently, as though working out an alternate launch vector: other causes are not so far-fetched. We know the Russians, the Koreans, the Brazilians all have the same technology, the same ships, the same nuclear launchpads that'll leave an uninhabitable area the size of the Dakotas behind each ship, the same on-board weapons systems that I've spent hundreds of hours honing my fluency in during afternoon video game sessions.

As the fields rush by, so alike in their differentness, I let myself think about the switched exercise. That's never happened before. The fact of these two out of the ordinary events coinciding in a single 24-hour period after two thirds of a year of sameness: it's hard to resist connecting them. Maybe there's been a political escalation? An assassination? A warning shot? So we're launching early? All plausible, I decide. But I can't know. Since last spring I've been in my tower, with no knowledge of the world outside. I have only the information I can touch, see, smell, think.

I let my brain be free again, switching off this train of thought. My tower appears as a dot in the distance, growing imperceptibly larger as I pedal. Yesterday's exercise, all the math problems of the last few weeks all start to fall into a pattern, something I can't quite grasp, like the memory of a taste. The road furls out ahead of me, my tower looming now, its clean industrial shape outlined against the sky. Not for nothing has my brain been honed for pattern recognition and mathematical precision. The solution comes to me in the moment that I can first see the door leading into the entrance shed—our trips don't all have to be one-way.

I hadn't seen it before, because of course there is no purpose in returning to a dying Earth. My training involves zero scenarios in which we would turn around part way through our journey. And certainly not once we've arrived at the paradise planet circling Alpha Regulus and discharged our human cargo, a generation born on-ship, piloted by my successor, who will be chosen and trained from those born aboard—I imagine her pedaling a stationary bicycle for an hour every morning, possibly while watching a video of this same scenery I see now. It's a one-way trip for the people of our nation, and all this training is to aid me in piloting them past all dangers and obstacles.

But all my training contains another possibility—given a difference in thrust, there is also a set of implied downward arcs, which my brain is now synthesizing, pinpointing their potential landing—or crash—spots. In major cities? I don't have the coordinates memorized. It's entirely possible.

The rush of adrenaline that hits me at this thought does not fade and my coping skills do not kick in. A metallic taste numbs my tongue, and my feet and hands are shot with sharp electric pinpoints where they contact the bicycle pedals and grips. It could be that all of us starpilots training in our towers, we could all be winners but not of the contest we hoped for. Did my dead rival come to this conclusion before her demise and pay the price? No, our keepers would not have ended her life in such a discoverable way. But perhaps she could have put a stop to her own trajectory, prevented her own return trip? Could I, should I do the same?

Or, I think, calming my breathing, it's entirely likely our rivals have learned of our strategy through spycraft. Before I entered training, there were spies being shot on the news every few months. I have always understood this risk, thrived on the idea of playing a bit part on the world stage. I would destroy the plains to magnanimously save the colonists of this nation, few of whom—I'm under no illusions—would look remotely like me. My great-grandmother and I, we rise above, we succeed, and we lead. I've come to terms with this. But would I destroy Manaus? Vladivostok? Most of the Joseon peninsula?

Of course I would, I think, a pit of nausea making itself known inside me. I would have no choice. I have sworn and I have trained. And I would have no way to know anyway, until far too late, if I were piloting a colony ship to the stars or a missile hurtling under insufficient thrust to reach orbit.

I've arrived at the tower and Clara has taken my bicycle, is helping me out of my down suit. Numb, the world at a distance around me, I carry on with my structured, familiar day, absorbing and remembering none of it.

The next morning, I feel much better—a product of the sleeping drugs as much as of my own psychological skills. I have shoved aside all my swirling thoughts and am determined to make the most of my training ride, to make the most of each remaining moment of my life. Downstairs, I smile at Clara and break protocol with a cheerful hello. She looks away, forehead creased.

That's when I see it. It's like I'm seeing her face for the first time. And not just her face; the entire world shifts in that moment. Clara looks nothing like me, nothing like the pale dead candidate, nothing like the thousands of starship colonists I'm training to ferry safely to a distant shore. She's one of the billions who are screwed either way; pulverized by my blast or by my landing or simply deprived of breathable air by the inexorable process of climate decay.

My heart is pounding. This is why we aren't allowed to interact with our attendants. How can I go about my structured days with this awareness of her humanity and how my actions will affect her?

Fortunately all I have to do now is get on my bicycle. I crave the escape, the movement, the chance to shake off this disturbing new vision and return to my orderly existence, for all it seems so far out of reach.

On the bike ride, before my consciousness even registers the slight movement from behind the small hillock to the left of the road, my body reacts. I hit the ground, tucking and rolling, screaming like a community safety siren, all before the sound of the silenced shotgun registers, the harsh, foreign oath.

Pressed against the ground, I turn my head to look up and see a dark figure fleeing.

My breath comes raggedly. I steady it. I can't think now. I pick up the bicycle and ride.

When I get to the crossroads, I sail right through as usual. Then I do something I've never done before, not in 218 of these rides—I hit the brakes.

Stopped, the world continues around me. Grass sways in the breeze. A distant cow lows.

I turn around and pedal slowly to the middle of the intersection, looking left and then right.

Other trajectories, other futures play through my brain. I have no idea where these roads might lead, but the one now to my left leads away from my assassin and away from my tower. Taking a deep breath, wielding all the training I've ever received, I square my shoulders to my handlebars, step on the pedal, and take aim for the unknown.

AT THE CROSSROADS

Elly Bangs

She makes the mistake of glancing up from her handlebars, past towers that loom like perfectly straight teeth around the gaping mouth of the beige sky of Planet One. The split second of lost focus is all it takes for her front wheel to slip and give off a blood-curdling squeal on the surgical surface of the road and send her down in a blur of motion and pain and force. She tumbles over the steel and sees the sky roll end over end. For a moment she lies still, stunned. Finally she hears Diego's voice cutting through the adrenaline haze.

"Oh shit, Callie! You all right?"

He starts to help her up, but she waves him away. She catches her breath and straightens her eyepatch. She finds herself bruised but mostly unscathed—but now there's a crowd gathering at the transparent barrier at the edge of the street. There are hundreds of people, all alike: every last one of them bald, male, pasty, six feet tall, dressed in formless white coveralls. All staring down at her with identical blank expressions, through identical gold irises.

It's in this moment that she fully grasps that this isn't Earth. Not the Earth she knows.

She twists her right leg a few times to make sure it's in working order, then rises to her feet.

The man from Planet One (Blask, she remembers) comes back down the road to stare at her through his own golden eyes while his riding partner waits further ahead. The faintest trace of a grin crosses his harsh, angular face.

"Not used to our roads," he observes.

"How the hell do you ride on this stuff?" Diego asks. As if to punctuate the question, he nearly slips on the polished metal. The sound of his cleats scraping on the surface makes Callie's skin crawl.

"How do you ride on surfaces with so many imperfections and heterogeneities?" Blask responds, sliding his hand over his hairless, bone-white scalp and that strange metal plate set in it. He turns and rides off again, muttering: "Welcome to Planet One."

Callie watches him go, nervously. She looks back down the metal road the way they came and sees the two riders from Dynnya, as much aliens as herself in this world, gradually catching up.

"Sure you're all right?" Diego asks.

"I'm fine. You know me." She glances up into the beige sky, trying to guess the size and distance of the knifelike, shadowy shapes that loom there. They must be miles long, those machines, and there are hundreds of them. Warships. Each is lined from end to end with guns or cannons or electrodes, like spines on some evil insect. She swallows hard and tries to sound calm when she says: "Come on. The sooner we make it to the next world, the better."

Diego chuckles. "What if the next world is even weirder than this? You don't know."

She takes a look around at the metal street, walled by plate glass or force fields or whatever it is, and feels as if she's in a zoo. A terrible, ominous feeling comes over her when she sees all those people watching her: it's as if they're laughing. Except it's even worse than that because somehow it's as if they would laugh, but can't—as if they lack that ability altogether. She shudders and says "It can't be weirder than this."

Diego glances around. "Shit, man. I've probably got more melanin in my body than everyone on this whole planet combined. You've probably got more in the tip of your toe!" He laughs nervously, then turns serious. "Hey. What did the Major say to you?"

"Huh?"

Diego's bike starts to shimmy on the metal, but he catches himself. "It looked like you were having a heavy conversation. Right before the starting line. You've been kind of tense ever since."

She knows she can't merely brush the question off, but the whole truth is more terrifying than she can fully process, let alone find the words to tell Diego. Instead she clears her throat and responds: "We've just ridden our bikes through a rip in the fabric of the universe and will have to ride through four more such portals before we reach the finish line. We are racing two teams of alien-people across four different planets in an attempt to somehow avert the apocalyptic interdimensional war we're all worried is coming. Tense? Yes, I am kind of tense!"

Diego hesitates and then adds: "You've got to admit this is pretty badass, though. Right?"

"There's something you need to understand."

"Yeah? What's that?"

Callie stares down the vanishing point of the gleaming metal canyon of Planet One to the two chiseled, pearlescent-plastic-clad backsides of the racers ahead of her, and tells her teammate: "We have to win."

"That's the general idea of a race, right?"

She glares at him, hard. "No. Listen to me, Diego. We have to win."

•　　　•　　　•

Two hours ago, Callie had been sitting in the shadow of a hangar, staring off into the distance and trying to collect her thoughts. Beyond the rusty gray of the hangars stood mesas of pinkish rock dusted with dry shrubs;

beyond them, an ocean of flat land spread out to the horizon, baking in the Summer sun outside Gallup, New Mexico, Earth—her Earth. Beyond that was the rip, and somewhere still farther off, unthinkably, was another sky. She knew she wouldn't be able to see it from here, but she couldn't stop trying.

She heard an engine rumbling somewhere and turned to see Major Case and his jeep come boiling out of a mirage on the tarmac. He stopped in front of her, waiting. It was time.

"I'm trying to remember how you convinced me to do this," she said.

"Honestly, I'm not sure. But I'm glad I did."

She reached for her leg with her good hand, sliding the prosthetic socket over the scar tissue below her right knee and adjusting its position several times before fiddling with the valve.

"Anxiety is natural," said Major Case, now gazing at a particular part of the horizon himself—he probably knew exactly where the rip was from here. "Only a handful of people have been where you're going. We don't know all of what you may find."

"It's not the danger that's got me anxious," she said, standing and testing her weight on the carbon fiber. "Mainly I just can't believe I'm working for you again. After all this time."

"You're not. Not really. You're an independent contractor. The Air Force is only here to organize the event and provide security on our side of the rip. This is a diplomatic effort." He sighed uneasily. "I know you'll keep that in mind when you speak with the other riders."

"On second thought, that's what I'm anxious about." She was pulling her mesh gloves on, pausing to flex her right hand as far as it would go, and smoothing her dreadlocks down under her helmet. "God, why is this happening? Why did Los Alamos have to go and tear the universe open?

Why can't they just patch it all back up? Seal the breaches? Fix their own damn mistake?"

"They're trying. Believe me. They've been trying since the rips formed."

"They're not going to finally work it out while I'm on the other side, are they? I'd hate to be stranded out there."

"Not likely. They still don't understand how they caused all this."

"But you really think this 'Ride of the Four Worlds' is going to make a difference? You think all this is going to prevent a war?"

"Sport can bring people together. A little structured, nonviolent competition can allow disparate groups to work out their differences and find common ground."

At that moment Diego shot out of the hangar and started riding tight circles around the Major's jeep, whooping excitedly. "Hey, let's do this! You ready, Cal? Saddle up! Things are about to get inter-dimensional!"

Callie smiled in spite of herself.

"Hey, Major!" Diego made an awkward attempt at a salute and eventually waved instead. "I just want to say what an honor it is to be doing this."

The Major nodded, stiffly. He'd desperately wanted to set Callie up with some squeaky-clean astronaut as a teammate—someone to present an appropriately dour attitude to the press—but she'd made it clear she wouldn't ride with anyone but Diego. The same upbeat humor that repelled the Major was something she'd come to rely on. (For his pride's sake, however, her contract stipulated that no one tell Diego any of this.)

The cyclists rolled after the Major's jeep, over the hot pavement and weeds, between the weathered concrete buildings of the base and down the tarmac to the starting line. Her heart raced as they approached the other two pairs of riders. She'd seen their photos, but there was something she understood in seeing them with her own eye: their being human didn't make them any less alien.

The men from Planet One looked like statues carved out of white marble. She knew their names were 059-Blask and 186-Hellgrow, but she couldn't tell them apart by sight. They both stood six feet tall with startlingly broad shoulders, and Callie thought she could see individual strands of corded pectoral muscle through the glossy white material of their clothes. They had no hair, not even eyebrows, and their irises were a blazing iridescent gold. Each seemed to have a metal plate set into the naked scalp above their right ears. Their bicycles looked more or less ordinary, except that the tubes were as thin and sharp as piano wires.

The other pair were from Dynnya: a tall, portly person named Luminastri and a short, thin one named Water. Callie couldn't guess at their genders, assuming they had genders. Each was wrapped in an asymmetric patchwork of green and brown material that was baggy in some places and form-fitting in others, seemingly at random. They both had long, braided black hair, full of bits of metal that glinted in the sun. Luminastri's skin was light-brown with large, darker spots, while Water's was nearly olive green. Their bicycles were thick and organic-looking. As Callie studied them she was sure she saw one flex very slightly, as if breathing.

·　　·　　·

Callie is initially relieved when she looks ahead down the metal-plated road and sees the rip in space that will lead her out of Planet One and into Dynnya, the third of the four worlds on the route—but when it's looming over her she can't repress a twinge of fear. Like the rip that took her between her own Earth and Planet One, it's roughly circular and about a mile in diameter, and it dances with distorted light and ghost images. Diego is right, she thinks, there's no way to know what waits on the other side. Not until it's too late.

"Here goes nothing," she says, and rolls through the rip.

This time she tries to keep her eye open. She sees the twisted mirror of reality slide liquidly around her, and then she's on the other side.

She feels the traction in the tires before anything else and finds herself on a dirt road stretching over lumpy hills covered in bluish grass. The landscape is peppered with trees and shrubs, but nothing she immediately recognizes as a building. The sky is pregnant with rain. Meanwhile the riders from Planet One are stopped and staring back from a short distance ahead, sticking up out of the sinuous dirt road like white fangs from a giant snake. Cautiously, the two riders from Earth move to catch up with them, just as they hear the Dynnyans rattle through the rip behind them. A vague, tenuous peloton forms—although the riders from Planet One stay at the front, speeding up whenever anyone else gets close enough to draft.

Diego keeps studying the other teams, passing glances ahead and behind. Finally he clears his throat and yells: "Common ground! We come from really different places, but we all ride bicycles! That's pretty cool, right?"

There is an awkward silence. Then Blask calls back over his shoulder: "The bicycle is simply the most efficient mechanism of individual transport."

"The bicycle is the last invention that brought nothing but happiness to humankind," one of the Dynnyans calls forward. Callie can hear the smirk in their voice. She turns and sees Water following close behind her.

"I just think they're fun," Diego says.

Blask shakes his head. His teammate glances back only briefly and continues to say nothing.

"Real talk," Diego says. "What do you all think is the relationship between the four worlds connected by the rips? Like, they're all the same planet, right? They're all Earth. But, like, in different dimensions?"

"Wrong," Blask calls back. He's looking straight over his shoulder, not apparently looking at the road at all, but his balance is unwavering. "The four worlds are the same planet at different points in time."

Diego scans the horizon. "So what, this is the distant past? Dynnya is some kind of prehistoric Garden of Eden that invented bicycles ten thousand years early? And my Earth is the present, and Planet One is the future?"

"Wrong," Blask says. "Planet One is the present. All the other worlds are the past."

"So if that's right," Callie calls out, "I guess what we Earthlings do, the choices we make in our present, decide the future. Our actions could change Planet One."

"Wrong," Blask says again. "That would describe a temporal paradox. A logical impossibility. The course of history is predetermined and unchangeable and it trends inexorably toward our world. Planet One is the apex and actualization of humankind."

"Interesting theory," says the Dynnyan named Luminastri.

Callie finds herself gnashing her teeth. She wants to ask whether there are any women on Planet One—or really anyone who isn't apparently an exact facsimile of Blask himself—but she's afraid to know the answer.

They ride on in a tense silence for a long time. The road takes them down into a valley full of small dry flowers of every shape and color. The air is clean and suffused with petrichor. When they reach the bottom and start climbing again, Callie looks back and sees the Dynnyans close on her tail again. There's language in their maneuvering, she senses—

the way they back off slightly when she turns, seemingly waiting for an invitation to come closer—that seems friendly, almost playful. In the warm sunlight, Water's greenish skin doesn't look sickly the way it did under the beige sky of Planet One; here it looks vivid. Beautiful.

"You're a warrior?" they ask.

The question catches Callie off guard. "A what? I mean… I was. I guess. For a while. Years ago." She swallows hard.

Water says nothing. They're studying her, but in a way that seems more curious than judgmental.

"Yes, that is how I got injured," she volunteers. "If that's what you're really asking. I was flying a plane, and it broke down. It crashed."

"A plane?"

"A flying machine. Like a… a big, fast, screaming metal bird."

"Your people fight wars with things like that?"

Callie sighs. "What, you don't have wars on Dynnya?"

"Nope," Water says.

"Never?"

"Nope."

"She must really like you," Diego tells Water, breaking the tense silence that follows. "That's more than she's told me about her past in all the years we've been racing together."

"It was a long time ago," Callie says. "I haven't been a 'warrior' in a long time. Not that kind of warrior anyway."

"Why not?" Luminastri asks, pulling in closer.

Callie sighs and twists her hands on the bars. "I was a lot younger. Head all full of good versus evil, us versus them bullshit. I really thought if we could just blow up all the evil-doers, the world, my world, would get better. Turns out I didn't know shit."

The peloton crosses over the top of a hill and starts down the other side.

"Hey, so, uh—" Diego shouts to the Dynnyans over the wind. "Are you two…? Are you men or women or what?"

The Dynnyans exchange glances with each other, blushing and grinning.

"What?" Diego asks. "Why are you looking at me like that?"

Water says "Where we come from, that question means… That is…."

"You only ask someone that when you want to sleep with them," Luminastri finishes.

"What? Really?" Diego laughs awkwardly. He hesitates and says "I mean, uh. So what if I am anyway?"

Callie reaches across and smacks him on the shoulder. "No diplomatic incidents, please."

The Dynnyans laugh louder.

Hearing the commotion behind them, the men from Planet One glance back. It's almost inaudible over the sound of the wind through the dry flowers, but Callie is sure she hears Blask mutter two words under his breath: Deviants, all.

· · · ·

"God speed," the Major had said, back on Earth, just before they parted.

Diego continued on to the starting line, but Callie hesitated. She stopped at the Jeep's side, studying the Major, certain there was something he wasn't telling her. Finally she said: "Why me, Case? You know I'm not the fastest rider on the planet."

"The fastest riders on the planet were too chicken. But even if they'd had the guts, this is no ordinary race. We need someone with an extraordinary ability to handle the unexpected and unknown. Someone who can crash over and over and always get back up again. You might be the best on Earth at that. It's what you're famous for."

"So you hired me because I crash."

"Because you know how to crash. How not to let it stop you. And because you've been trained to survive in extreme environments. And because you're a medalist. Your speed and endurance are phenomenal."

"Sure they are, but that's different from being the best. I'm not. Not by any numerical measure I know, speed or otherwise. But you chose me to go out there and represent the entire world?"

"Representation is exactly the point." He took off his cap and turned it contemplatively in his lap. "To be honest, I don't think there's a cyclist on Earth who could beat Blask and Hellgrow. But the government, all the governments of Earth, recognize that our participation in this event is a statement we're making to the other worlds, regardless of who wins. Who we choose to ride for us is a statement about who we are. As a species. As peoples."

"And what statement do you think I make?"

He squinted up at her and said "Defiance."

She added, somewhat derisively: "As your token one-eyed, one-legged black woman, you mean. I'm your symbol of defiance, huh?"

The major studied her silently for an awkwardly long moment. Finally he stared off into the haze and said, "I know I shouldn't tell you, but you deserve to know. There's… there's been a large military buildup on the other side of the rip. On Planet One. The consensus of the intelligence community is that they're massing for a simultaneous invasion of all three other worlds. Maybe next week. Maybe today. We've run numerous simulations and have come to the conclusion that, given their technological and numerical superiority, we can't expect to repel any such incursion. Not even by nuclear means."

Callie's jaw dropped. "…What about Dynnya? Can they…?"

"Everything we know about Dynnya tells us it's an extremely primitive world. Largely an agrarian economy. We think they have some sort of biotechnology, but as for the men and materiel required to fight a full-scale interdimensional war? They don't even have centralized governmental authorities. No standing armies of any kind. They won't be able to put up any more of a fight than the lifeless wasteland of the Fourth World will."

Callie was speechless.

"This may well be the end of our history," Case continued, distantly. "If it is, then who we send on this ride will be sort of like our epitaph, as a global civilization. It will speak to how we valued life. How we were different. How we treated our differences… or, at least, how we wish we had, before they were… taken from us."

"Taken?"

"You'll understand when you meet them."

．　　　　．　　　　．

"We shouldn't be here," Diego says, and his voice seems to echo eerily over the vast, empty dust of the Fourth World.

Callie says nothing. Her eye darts anxiously between the road ahead of her and the digital Geiger counter strapped to the top tube of her bike. Rationally she understands that the red glowing numbers in front of her are within safe limits, given the short length of time they'll all be here, but in her heart all she can see is their slow but inexorable upward march.

She takes a look around and thinks that if it weren't for the air and gravity, she might have thought she was riding on the surface of the moon. The sky is solid black with a few fuzzy tendrils of charcoal blocking out the stars. The sun hangs halfway up, surrounded by concentric rings of dirty haze. The ground all around them is a bleached white color, covered in a layer of bone-dry dust. Ash? There are no plants, no people, no buildings, no wind or sound—just, impossibly, a weathered but mostly intact two-lane highway stretching out from horizon to horizon. The monotony of the landscape makes depth perception even more of a struggle than it had been already.

The counter makes a soft blipping noise every few minutes. One rad. Two rads. Three.

"We really shouldn't be here," Diego repeats. "Something wrong with the air. Smells like death. Place just feels… wrong. Shit. We should not be here."

"Yeah, well," she says, "everywhere I've ever gone was somewhere somebody thought I shouldn't be. Including me, sometimes."

The land is so flat and the air so clear that she can see all the way to the last rip. It's a small, faintly glowing circle in the distinct distance, about twenty miles away. Its subtle fluctuations are the only motion in sight. Just on the other side is Earth, and the finish line.

"Seriously, what the hell happened to this world?" Diego asks. "Nukes?"

Callie cringes as the counter gives off another blip. "A lot of them. Or something even worse. A long time ago."

"Just what happens to a world when you try to fix it by blowing up all the evil-doers," says Luminastri.

"Could be," Callie says.

When she glances over her shoulder, the riders from Dynnya are watching her with a look of silent appraisal. She feels vaguely aware that something important is happening in their heads at this moment—but it's the two riders in front of her that have her attention.

Since the start of the ride she's been studying the men from Planet One, watching how they respond to different inclines and terrains, sometimes rushing at them to test their speeds. Their bodies are so strange, like old-fashioned Superman cartoons, and she knows there's a chance that everything she knows about fitness won't apply—but she's come to believe that they've trained for speed, not stamina. She knows she won't beat them close to the finish line, but out here? If she can use their sense of superiority against them, get them to wear themselves out rather than suffer the indignity of letting her pull ahead for even a moment....

She waves to Diego to bring him alongside her. In the years they've known each other they've developed a shared language of nonverbal cues. They know each other's mannerisms and body language in and out.

Are you ready to get out of this hell? she asks him with her eyebrows.

Are you kidding? He asks by way of a smirk.

Callie closes her eye. She takes a sip of water and feels its coolness move through her in a wave. She flexes her fingers on her handlebars, rotates her right wrist, feeling the screw in the bone. It's time. She takes a deep breath, stares dead ahead, furrows her brow, and summons her second wind.

The earthlings rapidly overtake the men from Planet One, squeezing around the edge of the pavement before they realize they're coming. Callie and Diego stay in the lead, pushing themselves to their limits and cutting aggressively from side to side to block Blask and Hellgrow from passing, but just for a minute—just to put the heat on them. It works. Callie pretends to let them through accidentally, then Diego slips back, and the two of them ride the men's huge aerodynamic wakes as they barrel over the ashy pavement at high speed.

"You can't win," Blask says irritably. "You might as well get that idea out of your head right now." He keeps veering sharply to the right, trying to force her to get out of his wake or risk colliding with him—a danger she's acutely aware of as she struggles to keep track of his distance in her good eye—but she stays there, using him as shelter for her wind resistance. Making him expend more energy than her on every foot they roll together.

You verbose fool, she thinks. If I can just keep you talking, maybe you'll finally run out of breath one of these days. She grins wickedly and shouts: "Doesn't Hellgrow ever talk?"

"Not in my presence," Blask says. "Obviously."

"Why's that obvious?"

"I am 059-Blask. He's 186-Hellgrow."

"So what, Blask?"

"'Blask' is not my name, it's merely a title. On Planet One, we don't have names. Instead, we each have a specific number. Each person's identifying number has thirty-two digits, though we only need the first three in most interactions. My number is far closer to zero than 186-Hellgrow's. I'm a series-zero, he's a series-one. Therefore, obviously, he does not speak unless I speak first. That's how everything works. That's the only way it can work."

How can he just keep rambling on like that without stopping to breathe? she thinks. He's barely even watching the road as he turns over his shoulder to talk to her—but he's not escaping her either. Keep at it.

Between breaths she says: "I don't get it."

"Of course you don't. Our people knew from the moment the portals opened that war was inevitable. You must understand that it's extremely jarring to even speak to you. It violates our social structures."

"What?"

"You have no numbers. And no neural regulators! We don't know how to interact with you. At first we had no idea how you could even interact with each other. Eventually we came to understand. Look, any kind of interaction between people depends on all participants knowing who is superior and who inferior. Right? Who serves who. Who commands and who obeys. Who speaks and who listens. Without that there's only animal chaos."

"What the hell? That's not true."

"Yes it is. You do understand this, even if you say you don't. Your world understands it. It's just that your system for doing it is hopelessly primitive. Savage, really." His golden irises twinkle eerily in the otherworldly light.

"What?!"

"On the first segment of this ride, back in your world, we passed by a demarcated place. What do your people call it? A 'reservation.' Its purpose is clear: to contain people whose identity-numbers would be, in Planet One terms, farther from zero. To establish who was inferior, and who superior, in an interaction. To take power from some and give it to others. That's well. The problem with your world is how unclear the entire thing is. You don't have just one hierarchy. You have dozens, hundreds of overlapping structures for establishing dominance and concentrating power. Male over female. White over black. Rich over poor. Able over damaged. As it should be, but for want of a unified structure it's hopelessly inefficient."

She feels her blood run hot and her knuckles go white on the bars. There's a different energy flowing through her now, powering her forward momentum—fury—but she worries that if she taps it fully she'll burn through all the stamina she's been saving for this, so she stuffs it down. She stays right in the middle of his wake. She pushes him faster. In her peripheral vision she sees Diego and Hellgrow, engaged in the same high-speed dance.

"My world has perfected all of that," Blask continues. "In our world, every man knows his place. There is never any confusion or conflict. Our numbers mean that any two people who may ever meet on Planet One, under any circumstances whatsoever, know immediately which of them is dominant in the interaction. And whenever someone's natural urge contradicts that order, that urge is neutralized before it can lead to chaos." He taps the gleaming metal plate in the side of his naked scalp.

"What happens to people like me on Planet One?" she asks.

Blask raises one hairless brow and shrugs. "It seems to me that there are many different things you might specifically mean when you refer to 'people like you', but the answer is the same in any case. There are no people like you on Planet One."

·   ·   ·

"That's it?" she'd said, back on Earth. "You're just going to tell me all that and send me off as if everything's peachy?"

Major Case rather brazenly opened the jeep's glove compartment and pulled out a half-empty bottle of whiskey. When he sighed she could smell it on his breath. He said, "Foreknowledge of death is an interesting thing. I find myself… driven to atone for my misdeeds. I withheld the truth from you once before. When you served under me. I knew about the mechanical issues with your A-10 that led to the crash. I downplayed the risks. I was covering my own ass."

It should have meant something to her to hear, but she felt oddly numb. "I know that. I knew it then."

"Well, now I'm confessing." He took a furtive swig. "Truthfully, I've never stopped thinking about it. Losing sleep over it. I couldn't withhold the truth from you again. I feel I owe it to you."

A hot wind blew over the weeds and cracked concrete of the base. Callie looked around the sky, at a loss. "Whose idea was this race?" she asked, dazed. "Yours?"

"An envoy from Dynnya proposed"—he hiccupped—"the whole thing. At the time it seemed like a good idea. Now it's the only idea we have left."

"I feel my own idea coming on."

"Listen, I know… maybe you wouldn't have agreed to do this if you'd known. And I know you're thinking of leaving now. You could get on a bus home and I wouldn't be able to stop you. But I remember you, Callie. I know who you are, and I know you'll do this ride because in your heart you understand that you and Mr. Selva are in a unique position here. You get to compete with them. You get to fight, in your own way. Up against Planet One's weapons, the rest of us won't even get that chance."

"Fight? How the hell can we fight them?"

"If anyone can figure that out, I believe it will be you."

She and the Major shared one more long silence, and then there was nothing left to do but ride.

·　　·　　·

The last rip in spacetime is growing in her vision. She glances back and judges they're about five miles from the midpoint between the two. She knows she's running out of time to make her tactic work.

"And that's what you'll do to us if you win the race?" she shouts.

"Obviously we'll introduce our hierarchy on Earth—Planet Two—regardless of the outcome of the race. But if I win the race I'll be promoted to series-049. I'll be awarded reproductive privileges." He smiles. "Even if I were not superior to you in every way, for that reason alone you could never win. I have more to gain by winning than you ever could. But, in any case, our participation in this event is merely a delay tactic. The invasion will commence very shortly."

"How shortly?"

"Seventeen minutes from now."

She gives Diego one last look, just to read his expression and know he's heard everything.

"Fuck it," she says, and pushes ahead through Blask's wake.

He tries to ram into her as she shoots past him, but he's too late. She's in front of him.

"No!" he yells. "Impossible!"

"Eat my dust, Nazi!" she yells without turning.

She holds nothing back now. She taps the full force of her rage, her fear, her desire, her pride, her love of her entire planet and everything she knows, and keeps pushing herself harder and harder into the distance.

"This changes nothing!" Blask yells. "Even if you were to win—" She hears him panting now. "—Which you will not—it changes nothing. We will take Planet Two. We'll pave the whole thing over! It will all be—" He struggles to catch his breath. "—Erased! It will all be forgotten!"

"You'll remember me," Callie yells.

"No!"

He roars. She can hear the rhythmic hiss of his breath through the lifeless, irradiated wind of the Fourth World, coming closer. She doesn't dare to look back but she knows he's right there, and then something snaps hard, too fast for her to react, and—

She falls.

This time she goes down hard and at high speed. Her eye catches flashes of the bike swinging end over end through the empty black sky and flying off in the direction of the sun, and her body rolls on its side through streamers of soft, bone-white, radioactive ash.

She lies still in the dust for what seems like a long time, catching her breath and waiting for the shakes to pass, listening to Diego shouting her name until she answers. She wiggles the toes of her foot and mentally checks herself for any breaks or sprains or dislocations, but finds none. Finally she lets him help her sit up. When she opens her eye, she sees all the other riders stopped, watching her.

"You shoved her right off the road!" Diego shouts at Blask. "I saw you do it!"

"Yes," Blask says simply.

Diego starts toward him as if to start a fight, but Luminastri grabs his shoulder.

"We have to go back now," they say. "The race is over."

"You're damn right it's over. I'm gonna kill—"

"No. Look." Water is pointing at something. At first Callie can't figure out what, but then she realizes: the rips. Water is pointing at the portals on either end of the long empty road. The light around their edges is pulsating unevenly now, and from here Callie can see the shape distorting, bending inward, like a whirlpool around a bathtub drain.

The rips are sealing themselves.

"What?" Callie gapes. "How is that…? Los Alamos finally figured out how to patch them up? Now?"

"None of us want to be stuck here in the Fourth World," Luminastri says. "We should have just enough time to reach the portal back to Dynnya before it shuts forever." "But… what about Earth?!" Diego gasps. "You're saying we'll be stuck there forever?"

Without another word, Blask and Hellgrow take off again, headed for the finish line.

"You won't make it in time!" Water calls after them. "It's much too far away! You'll be trapped here!"

But the men from Planet One are already gone.

"Can you ride?" Luminastri asks, hurrying to Callie's side.

Her hip, shoulder and hands are scraped nearly raw and bleeding through a thick layer of white ash. She doesn't realize the prosthetic was ripped away in the crash until Luminastri hands it to her. She winces and struggles to reattach it.

"I saw the way you fell," the person from Dynnya says. "If that had been a leg of flesh and bone it would've been snapped in half."

"Lucky me."

"Your bike still rolls," Diego says. "But your wheels are kind of bent, handlebar's sideways, and your right brake lever snapped clean off."

"I don't think we'll need brakes for this part," Callie says, and stands. She mounts the crooked bicycle, ignores the pain, and pushes the pedals down. The four of them hurry for the rip as fast as they can.

It shrinks before Callie's eye the whole way. When the four racers reach it it's only as wide as the road. There's no time to slow down: they dive in.

Callie narrowly avoids crashing for the third time when she rattles through to the other side. She's not prepared for what she sees: the blue-green hills are now lined with people, and there's something huge looming in the sky directly above the dirt road. It looks like a bubble of space, roughly polyhedral, beating like a heart, bending the sunlight in kaleidoscopic patterns. The bubble-thing is held aloft by what looks like four huge green balloons, like the throats of giant frogs caught mid-croak.

"What the holy hell is that thing?!" Diego shouts and nearly crashes.

Luminastri lays their bike down. They approach him carefully and put their hand softly on his shoulder.

"It's okay," they say. "Try to stay calm. Diego? Earth is safe. We detected that Planet One had started its invasion, so we closed all the portals. Everything will be okay."

"You closed them," Callie echoes in disbelief.

Luminastri meets her gaze and then looks at their feet, somewhat guiltily.

"You were the ones who opened them in the first place," Callie says. "It wasn't some Los Alamos particle accelerator experiment gone awry at all, was it? It was you cutting holes in the fabric of the universe all along."

Water nods.

More Dynnyans approach Callie with what might be medical supplies, but she pushes them away. She drops her shattered bike and glares at the racers. "You lied to us."

"Only by omission," Luminastri says with a placating gesture. "We never said we hadn't created the rips, or that we couldn't control them. But… admittedly, we knew both Earth and Planet One would assume it was beyond our capabilities."

"Why?" Diego asks. "Why open the rips in the first place? Why do all of this?"

Water and Luminastri exchange pensive glances and motions, as if negotiating which one of them will explain.

"Better if we just show you," Luminastri finally says, waving to the Earthlings to follow them. "Besides, it's starting to rain."

They follow Luminastri and Water over a near hill and down a smaller path, out of sight of the dirt road. All around them, Dynnyans of all sizes and colors and shapes watch them pass and increasingly follow along, until they're surrounded by a whole crowd of onlookers: faces of greenish, reddish, bluish skin in countless organic and geometric patterns, full of curiosity and traces of awe. A warm rain falls and soaks Callie to the bone, washing away the blood and ash—and up ahead there's another rip, only ten feet in diameter, this one suffused with yellowish light.

"The four worlds are not different points in time, like Blask believed," Luminastri says. "They're all alternate versions of the same present."

Callie shakes her head. "But Dynnya and Planet One have such advanced technology. You both must be a thousand years ahead of us."

"In many ways, your Earth is taking its time," Luminastri answers with a smirk and stops just at the edge of the rip.

Unlike the bigger rips, this one is perfectly clear. From where they stand they can gaze straight through it like a window onto a high overlook above a grassland. Callie can feel the hot light on her palm when she shields her eye from the sun shining through the portal. There are towers scattered about, taller than she can guess: narrow, organic complexes of rooms and windows worming their way into the sky. Now Luminastri gesticulates to the rip and it shifts instantly to another view: a stretch of open ocean at dusk or dawn. There are objects suspended above the water, with narrow roots stretching down below the dark waves: crystalline, almost biological. These too have windows, and their jointed segments are knotted with clusters of rooms, spires, balconies, wind turbines, small gardens. Luminastri keeps feeding the portal hand signals, and it keeps cycling through vistas.

"All of this is Dynnya?" Diego asks.

"Dynnya is not just one planet. It's an alliance of 2,941 different incarnations of Earth—all those that have converged toward an end state in which all people are equally valued. This particular planet, the ground under our feet right now, we call the Crossroads. From here we can tunnel into tens of millions of different worlds. We study them. Sometimes we make contact.

"In all our explorations, we've learned that there have always been two contradictory natures in humanity. Equality and oppression, if you like. Freedom and control. Kinship and hierarchy. They exist in an uneasy tension: In nearly every world we've encountered so far, one of those natures has overwhelmed the other. Sometimes the world obliterates itself in the process of deciding. Others are much like Planet One, and still others are dead planets like the one you just saw. And then there's your Earth. Stubbornly refusing to make up its mind."

"Between what? Planet One and… you?"

"You've evolved differently than we have," Water says. "We can't tell you what's in your world's future. The things that worked for us may not work for you. In all of Dynnya there are no governments, not as you know them. By Earth standards most of our worlds don't even have a concept of private property."

"You don't have wars," Callie says.

"Not in many thousands of years. Like preventable disease, like hunger, like poverty, we realized we didn't need them."

"You still haven't answered my question," Callie says. "Why do all this? Why open the rips between the four worlds? Why the race?"

Luminastri turns away from the rip and looks at Callie seriously. Their eyes are lit by sunlight on an ocean. "Whenever two worlds collide, many things tend to happen. Some are terrible beyond words, but some are indescribably beautiful. This was our attempt to create the one without the other. One brief instance of contact before we seal the rips between Dynnya and Earth for another thousand years."

"So that we could all learn from each other," Water says. "For each world to see its reflection in the other three, and in doing so, know itself better. That was our hope."

"For Earth to know that it's not alone," Luminastri finishes. "So you could know that we see you. That we know you're going through a hard time, but… that we're here, and we believe in you. That someday you'll be ready to join Dynnya too."

Diego asks, "And now that it's over, what. Are we stuck here forever?"

"You can go back to your Earth whenever you want, but we hope at least one of you will stay a while and learn more about us and teach us about you."

"But we can go home right now if we want to," Diego says. "Right?" He looks at Callie, waiting for a nonverbal cue.

"Do you want to?" Water asks. The whole crowd of Dynnyans surrounding them seems to be asking the same question, silently, expectantly.

Callie looks around and decides. She takes a deep breath and closes her eye.

.   .   .

The six racers waited at the starting line, awkwardly: each pair so human, and at the same time so utterly alien to the others. They exchanged careful looks with each other, but there were no handshakes, no introductions. There was no etiquette for this. Everyone was too busy sizing each other up, or trying to perceive how theythemselves were being sized up.

Everything okay? Diego asked with a raised eyebrow, sneaking glances at the others.

Callie focused on her breath and tried to clear her mind. She nodded, fine, though there were many things she wanted to tell him. There were many things she was feeling all at once as she stared ahead down the empty highway that would take her away from Gallup until it took her away from the Earth itself. She wanted so much to turn to him and ask, point-blank: Do you feel it too? Like maybe you won't be coming back from this? And are you haunted, more than that, by an intuition—

A timer was counting down to the start of the race. Three, two, one.

—That maybe that wouldn't be so bad after all?

GENERATIONS

Osahon Ize-Iyamu

The First

Earth was a friend turned enemy. Normally, Ivie would have stayed back, faced the storm or whatever toxic life man had created over the years to make earth so unlivable. Five years ago, her decision wouldn't have been a question. What was the point of going to a new place?

"This one does not concern me o," her grandmother had said as Ivie packed her things, giving her that look, her grandmother crossing her arms in silent judgement. "Am I not still breathing, eh? The enemy that has been shouting I will die since has not reached me yet."

Ivie had gotten up and stared the woman in the eye. It was easier for her grandmother to say that when she had one foot in the grave, with nothing else to consider but herself. She was allowed to be stubborn.

"Apparently radiation hasn't reached this sector yet."

Grandma stretched her lips. It was funny; the old woman trying to persuade her to stay. "There's radiation there, too."

Ivie's mind flashed to the skin lesions she'd seen on her friend's back earlier in the week, the stories her husband had told her to convince her. "It's not as bad."

Her grandmother proceeded to shrug, pacing around. "I still think it's a money scam sha, but you are free. Even if it is true, I am not afraid of death. Let me go and practice my coding." Her grandmother left, the last Ivie would see of her, the final words.

Should she stay or should she go?

Ivie ended up with her husband nearby, one of his brown, hairy fingers intertwined with hers as she held their baby closer to her chest in the very last row of the very last spaceship, cramped for space and near the toilets. There were no seats available to soothe her back or place her child, sailing through the cosmos strapped to the wall with the other latecomers, as they all went up.

It wasn't comfortable, but it was something. And besides, the sacrifice wasn't for her. She was as good as dead for all she cared.

The jolt and toilet smell made her baby cry as well as other small children; fat tears through the silence, and the pressure of her chest. Nobody was talking, each to their own in a probable silent prayer for a safe journey. Ivie didn't pray; there was nothing else she could think to say that hadn't been said already. She didn't sleep, but she wasn't sure any grown adult would be. Everyone in the back looked stiff as a board, trapped till the end of the journey, silent as mice.

After all, who wanted to die after coughing up enough money to restart their life, then crash on the way?

No windows, but a harsh announcement slapped everyone out of prayer.

"Welcome to Mars."

It wasn't a sightseeing trip. Besides, there was nothing to see, just a large expanse of red earth, like how her father's farm looked like when he just bought it and it was full of opportunity. The stars were pretty but it wasn't enough. Ivie was sure she saw the dust of the air mix with the cold, the otherworldly nature of the dark sky of space, but the picture of this new world still didn't do it for her. It wasn't earth.

Beauty cannot be found here. Return back and you'll see it.

But my baby can't die. Not yet.

Sure, they had done their best to renovate it, make it look presentable, market and package it as a symbol for rebirth; but call a spade a spade. Try as hard as she could, she saw red land, back night. And a litter of stars.

"Isn't it beautiful?" Her husband tapped her, getting off the ship, clutching himself and shivering, his hair looking tangled and messy; his voice weird and funny from the hours of silence; even stranger when he took his first breaths through his oxygen regulator.

Ivie looked up again for the beauty. Maybe she had been missing something? Looking up, constellations of stars paved their way through black space, blinding lights through the night. They were better, but it felt like staring at the sun, sometimes magical, but only in small doses.

Then the cold. Her clothes didn't do enough to protect her, and like a battering ram, it hit her. Her teeth chattered, slamming against each other for some kind of warmth.

Moving was already the biggest jump she had taken. She couldn't afford to go jumping around from planet to planet. That wasn't life. All her life she had grown up in the same place, lived near each member of her family. And none of them had agreed to leave. Her family would move on. They would play games and host traditions, do the best of living before earth toppled on them.

Absence would not make their hearts grow fonder—distance, distance, distance. A million miles away. There would be no calls, no letters, no love.

Just tell yourself they're dead. It'll make you feel better.

That was how she saw it. Quick and swift and in the middle of the night. No explanation, nothing to be done. A time for mourning, and crying, then she was done. Thinking about their bodies, dying from radiation, collapsing and shrieking, riddled with scars. No. It was too much. It hurt, and her hands ached from holding her baby so long. She didn't have to care about herself. Just that her baby got everything, got opportunities.

Moving on.

Ivie took a deep breath, staring at her husband. "How are we sure we won't mess this place up again?"

Her husband whispered in her ear, his breath hot against her skin. "Hopefully, that won't happen for a very long time."

Ivie stretched her body. The only advantage of her seating position was that they got to come out first, before all the others: the politicians and presidential figures that booked first seating, abandoning earth. Also, funnily, the ones that missed the chance to sneak onto the American spaceships. Ivie stared at them, judged them as they came out, her face deep in a scowl.

You will not take your corruption here. Maybe in the new system of politics there would be an overhaul, and all things would work for good, and the future would be bright.

The landing spot for the Ghana and Nigeria spaceship looked nothing like the pictures she'd seen in the adverts. But then again, it was all about packaging. She gritted her teeth to the point where she wouldn't have been surprised to see her canines as stubs, having formed fresh white powder. Ivie bet her money that the fleet of spaceships designed for Americans and Brits landed somewhere much different.

But that's just the way it goes.

A man came to them, seemingly out of nowhere, a goofy smile plastered on his face.

"Welcome! Welcome, how was your journey? I'm Simon, your nearest consultant. You have any problems, you come to me."

Mostly murmurs were given as replies. The other people coming out bumped into her without apologies, moving their way to the front, relegating her to the back again. Snobs. Her husband wouldn't think much of it, but she knew better.

The white man looked like a tour guide or a front-desk clerk at a hotel. That only made her feel worse. She wasn't coming here to visit. How was your journey? Wasn't enough. Not in the slightest.

She stared at some people fiddling with metal parts or objects. Every large mechanical device that needed to be carried—cars, hoverboards— had to be broken down into junkyard scraps to rebuild later—pieces of a new life.

"Well, right this way," the man said. He did the tour guide thing again. Her belly tightened, looking around the desert place. Was this a mistake?

The man took them round, and she felt like she was moving in circles— practically floating due to the lack of gravity. Endless same paths to the same place—the definition of problems. Let's get lost, Ivie thought.

The tour guide found his way though and stopped after a while, stretched his hands out theatrically. There were a bunch of tents set up, like they were going camping.

"Welcome to your new home!" He shouted.

Ivie felt a drop of pressure in her stomach, like how she lurched when landing, like she would be thrown out of seat. Home? Tents. Tents? Home. What billows in the wind, barely tethered to the earth, barely protecting her from cold—tents.

And it was nonsense. She wouldn't take it. Her definition of home for her baby is the grandest place imaginable, space and space and space, land that children will inherit and fragment and give. Home must be great if she's come all this way, if she's left the whole galaxy and family and culture she's not sure she'd be able to experience again, and it couldn't be tents. If she went all this way to see home broken and redefined, to have traditions aching in her chest, pained from the distance, then she wouldn't be given the wrong end of packaging. She wouldn't be given what the general public's eyes didn't see.

Carrying her baby in her other hand, Ivie readied herself.

"This place is so small. Do you expect both Nigerians and Ghanaians to live here?"

Simon scratched his head. That could have meant uncertainty. That didn't sit well with her. Incompetence wasn't to be tolerated. "Well, as you know, we weren't nearly ready to live here before the radiation came, so this isn't exactly the fini—"

"And this place is…" she stomped her feet, annoyed at the imbalance. Her child would not run on a tilted terrain. She'd given up everything; she wasn't here to see mediocrity. The pause did make it seem like she was looking for complaints, which she was, but that wasn't the effect she was going for. Ivie ended her statement swiftly. "Too rocky. We've been moving past level landscapes since. Why is our home like this?"

Her husband slipped his hands into hers and Ivie took it, making a united fist. At this time, most of the other passengers were looking back at her, some raising their own questions in low voices.

She would not stay silent.

Simon scratched his head again, his smile still lingering, his words coming out with the same cold stare, rehearsed, not natural like before.

"Look, ma'am, many third world countries have—"

She squeezed her husband's hands a bit too tight, a jolt running through her. "We are not third world countries."

Simon sighed, taking a moment to pause and stare at her. She wouldn't allow him to win the conversation. This wasn't funny.

What is home? Home is not here.

"As I was saying, ma'am, many developing countries received land that has not finished being operated on, but of course that will change very soon." He used developing almost sarcastically, but she took it as a win. God knows she needed one at the moment. It made her belly untie some of its knots, made her breathe.

Others started to voice their concerns, then made their voices louder. She didn't think she was some kind of revolutionist, leading the way for others; she just wanted to know how things would be done.

By the looks of things, very poorly.

"And when will that be?" another person said.

Simon brought out his phone and slid through the projections. His cheeks turned red and he stuffed his phone back in his pocket. "There's still a lot of work to be done, you see? Of course, I don't expect anything longer than about two to three years."

"Years?" Someone at the back shouted.

"Yes," Simon nodded, looking increasingly weary with each question. It pleased her that she had tired him out. "So, in your houses—"

"Tents," she corrected him, stretching out the word so he could understand how unacceptable the situation was.

"My contact is in your phones, as well as a holographic map and address to my office. There's a satellite there for connection, but it dies some so it might take some adjusting to your devices in this new place. I'll let you settle in." Simon scurried away, the words fast and breathless, in a hurry to leave the conversation.

Ivie stared at the place again. The tents swayed from side to side with the dusty winds, but she hoped, prayed, they wouldn't fall apart. Adjusting the oxygen regulator they had given her before she'd left, she allowed spikes of fresh air to flow within her.

The spaceship went away, probably to park itself with the other ships, and she swallowed the fat lump in her throat. There was no going back. She was stuck here. Now she knew it. Shuffling feet made the best of a situation as people moved to their quarters.

"Don't worry," her husband whispered, the best he could without too many people hearing them. "If there's one thing Nigerians know how to do, it's fight for property. We will expand."

We will expand.

·   ·   ·

The Second

Adesuwa walked home because no one came to take her from school. It usually happened if Mummy and Daddy were busy digging for metals and ores during the day at the organisation. The days when Mummy was free, she went to Simon's office holding a signboard, her face stern, though Mama didn't speak much about that. Adesuwa felt sometimes her parents forgot about her, falling back to their beds and sleeping, too tired to do anything.

Adesuwa didn't mind walking, but she wished she could move. Seeing people fly past her on supercharged motorcycles made her feel electric, even if she wasn't the one riding.

She used to force both her parents to run around and play tag and toss with her, but these days, she let them sleep. Adwoa was a more willing partner anyway, but sometimes her friend only wanted to play tag, and there were other games. You mixed it up a bit, not just the same thing everyday. At least that was Daddy and Mummy's advice when they taught her how to cook her first meal.

"It's not jollof, but it will do," Daddy had said, giving her a smile that made him seem like he was in pain.

"What's that?" She had tilted her head to the side, falling out of her drumming skit with the big spoon.

"Never mind," Mummy replied quickly, and that was that.

But upon getting home, both of them were awake, listening to something. They were not smiling.

"What's happening?" She asked, laughing, hoping it would make the two of them smile.

"Everyone is dead," Mummy said, voice sharp, and something pinched Adesuwa's chest. She tried to grab at her mother's cloth, but Mummy pulled herself away, sharply, not to be touched, hitting Adesuwa in the process. She watched as her mother left the room, slamming the door behind her.

"What happened?" Adesuwa asked, her voice low, head spinning. Sharp pain spiked her shoulder. Her arms were still reaching out so for a minute Adesuwa thought what was wrong was due to the uncomfortable feeling that had settled in her house, like evil had come to rest. Evil that made her mother cold, unreachable, behind slammed doors. Evil that made her ache, causing pressure to tighten around her, making her not breathe. But then Adesuwa looked down, seeing that she forgot to regulate oxygen, and adjusted the device, causing her to receive a sharp intake of air, like hands finally removed from her neck.

"You should go to bed," Daddy said. He carried her, switching off the radio, but not before...

A sad event as we mark the end of Ear—

Adesuwa's eyes widened. She gave a look to her father, but he shut his eyes tight, as if holding something back. Even as Daddy settled her onto bed, when Adesuwa tried to speak, he shook his head. He closed her mouth. He shut the bedroom door and left Adesuwa in silence and black walls, where evil did not seem so far-fetched.

And the issue, like most things— they did not speak of it.

.   .   .

The First

Ivie sat down near the table, feeling the vase that looked like the most expensive thing the Ghanaian family owned. Their house was cramped, uneven, but not any more cramped than hers, but a step above tents, right?

We will expand.

She believed the statement less and less.

Yaa entered the room, staring at her.

"We never talk," the woman said, raising an eyebrow, looking straight into her eyes.

"But our daughters are friends. And..." Ivie paused, mastering it for great effect. "I want to talk."

"About what?" Yaa took a seat, crossing her legs.

How could Ivie process these emotions? How could she begin to talk about herself, and all the things she felt, and how she ached. To bring up Earth was an ache, a shattering against her rib, a stab. There was comfort in knowing, in the smallest part of her mind, that her family was living out all her old traditions, but now they were gone. And she couldn't just let all of their—her traditions die on earth. But Ivie was dead, not open for a new world, but she had to open up an old world for her daughter.

"I can't seem to talk about it. Culture, I mean. It feels like such an earth thing, and we're in this new place." Ivie noticed the woman's look after she said new. Well, earth was alive for a while, so new for planets could be a thousand years for all she cared. She stood by her statement. Besides, it wasn't her home. She thought when she first arrived that it was just skepticism, that it would pass, that all she needed was time to love the place.

Nope. It was all about her daughter.

"You know there's this new sort of pidgin all of them are speaking now, like they mixed our own with Mars slang," Ivie laughed nervously, smiling at the woman. "I needed to talk to someone. I don't know if you're doing better, but I can't keep up. And for someone, I want her to know that there was once a place different from here. Everything feels so much better and improved that it's kind of overwhelming."

Yaa put her finger in her own hair, softly stroking it as she spoke. The woman had a soft voice, like warm butter spreading on soft bread. It was part of the reason why she had come to her.

"I find that there are two cultures. Many of them don't really understand Earth, or any concept of tradition, so you just have to force it in. You can't let things fall out of place. If you do, there will be no history, no appreciation for the things that came before." Yaa stared into her eyes, voice soft but cool, almost steely. "Don't let it slip away."

~~We will expand.~~

Don't let it slip away.

·   ·   ·

The Second

"Why do we protest?" Adesuwa asked as Mummy readied her signboards with Daddy. It wasn't the first time she'd asked the question, but her mother had taught her that if you repeated something enough times, you could break the person.

"Unfulfilled promises, breach of contracts, for Simon to do his damn job and make sure someone cares about us enough so we don't end up being taken apart for more American malls and British museums..." Mummy listed each off her fingers, turning to smile at her. "Don't you worry about it! How do we know our home? By rocky ground. What do we always say?"

We will expand.

"Well, can I go too? I can make signboards and—"

"Absolutely not," Daddy cut in. "Why don't you go hang out with Adwoa?"

"She's sick," Adesuwa muttered, folding her arms. "Her mother said something about spaces getting cramped leading to sickness and epidemics... I wasn't really listening. Please, can I go?"

Both of her parents shared a look—they never told her anything.

If anything, they went faster.

·   ·   ·

The First

Ivie bought the bicycle scraps from the engineer next door. The misshapen things, rusted little relics of dead earth, gave her that feeling of nostalgia, reminding her of that weird other life she'd been living before she came here. She was different now.

"Madam, are you sure you want this one?" The engineer stared at her. She sighed. It wasn't easy running a local business in a place that was constantly reducing, fighting for space, clustered up in the middle of place called nowhere when it was her place, the home they'd given her.

The home they were practically trying to take away, bit by bit.

Buying something new would have given the woman more profits. She considered it, but wasn't in the position for reckless spending.

Ivie paid a little more, wincing as she folded the money, thinking of the extra hours she would put in at the mines. She nodded back at the woman, leaving her to count her blessings.

But what she'd gotten; it was everything.

It was also a distraction. She didn't need her daughter getting involved with whatever was going on. There were other things Adesuwa could be doing. Ivie thought about the mix of the two things, reasoned to herself how the reasons clashed, yet made the same noises—for love and protection.

It could be both.

•   •   •

The Second

For her birthday, things were different.

Waking up, she rushed outside, expecting that Mummy would mash together a nice cake and biscuits, even if it was the cheap ones that tasted like sand. She had learnt that not everyone got nice things, but even the cheaper things could be somewhat as good.

She stood in front of rows of food she had never seen before, her parents' clothes different from their usual colors, with more patterned fabrics decorated on it.

"What is this?" She raised an eyebrow, stretching out a lip, staring around. No cake, not even the cheap kind.

Mummy smiled, it was the first time she had in a while. "This is your culture."

She sat down and shrugged, tasting the food, both parents staring at her, waiting for her opinion.

"I…" she paused for her effect, as she'd learned from Mummy, shifting the food from cheek to cheek, letting the taste spread all over. "…like it!"

Her parents laughed, and she joined in too, because laughing was infectious. Also, because laughter was a remedy for when you didn't know what else to do.

"We really didn't plan this party well," Daddy whispered.

"Abeg, we'll just invite Adwoa over," Mummy said. Then she looked at Adesuwa, smiling. "Time for your gift."

Going back into the house, Mummy brought out a dull, rusted piece of metal. In some ways, it resembled the sleek motorcycles that people went around on, but like an unfinished form; like a first generation computer.

"It's a bicycle," Mummy laughed, but it wasn't funny. Adesuwa frowned, folding her arms.

"It looks like it's about to fall apart," she looked to her father. "Maybe we can trade it for something else, eh?"

"What nonsense!" Mummy screamed, and she jumped back, almost falling to the floor. "Let me tell you what we are going to do. We are going to renovate this thing, blend the old with the new. How do we know our home? By rocky ground. Earth and Mars."

Earth. And Mars.

•   •   •

The First

It was about learning how to do things, not just going about life with a simplified version of something. The motorcycles on Mars were nothing like an actual bike. No training needed in the slightest.

Every kid learns how to ride a bicycle. They just don't take this long to do it.

"Adesuwa," she screamed, rubbing her eyes. "You can't be afraid to fall."

"Never," her daughter shook her head. "I don't like injuries. Or pain."

"But," Ivie sang. Singing made the place feel less small, gave room where walls closed and left her alone. "That's the only way you can ride."

"Everywhere is so bumpy. It makes it harder."

"And that," Ivie nodded, "will make you stronger. Again."

Adesuwa rolled her eyes and sighed, throwing both feet to the pedals, moving slowly at first, then picking it up, moving faster, faster, faster.

"I'm doing it!" Adesuwa shouted.

"You're doing it!" Ivie screamed, jumping up, almost touching the stars. Ivie's heart swelled up, broke open, beating against the stars. Her daughter. Her champion. On rocky ground. Her most prized posse—

And then Adesuwa fell flat on her face to the uneven floor.

"Alright, let's move on to brakes."

Ivie felt calm, that she could be a mother and a fighter. That she could keep her daughter away from the troubles of protest and marches, let her be in that moment, riding in peace.

Let Adesuwa be blissful and ignorant, be kept away, hidden under the floorboards while the revolution went on.

We will expand.

. . .

The Second

Many years later…

It was a bicycle. Or a motorcycle. Both, but that wasn't the point. It moved: crackled and spurted, zipped with electricity, vibrating with power, a small Nigerian flag hanging for good luck.

Earth. And Mars. A little bit of both.

She was still that little girl—still moving, still moving. But she would not fall. The crowd stirred, millions of faces lost between dark and light under a million stars, each contestant one beating heart representing a nation. Adesuwa looked to the crowd, never ending, and felt a rush of familiarity.

A loud voice raised everyone's cheers, almost drowning within the sea of voices.

Welcome to the Olympics.

Speed is your friend.

Adesuwa balanced herself, her heart screaming from the voices of the crowd.

Silence. Just pretend they're all dead. You're moving, you're progressing. It'll make you feel better.

The track before her promised a lot of things. A long path. A hard race. Individual tracks demarcated by white chalk.

A gun shot, the kind designed for the power of Mars, so it struck the air with force.

Progression.

Adesuwa screamed, oxygen regulator to the fullest, riding purely on adrenaline, blood boiling several degrees. Moving. Moving. Moving.

For her trainer. She sped past the first track, past leagues of her others. Pressure. Pressure. Training flashed through her mind like a montage; the work of twelve weights a day, five hours of cardio, two hours of simulated attack sequences.

It will make you stronger.

For her parents. Her mother's spirit flowed through her, riding with her, goading her on. She looked back. There was no one ahead. She was first.

The way it's supposed to be.

Adesuwa grinned, upped the ante, moved at reckless speed. She could handle the accelerator. She could handle the brakes. She would win.

But she stopped, looking down at the tracks. The intersection. Rocky ground.

Her eyes widened. She covered her mouth.

How do we know our home? Earth and Mars?

Rocky. Ground. Here. Here. It'd been a long time since she'd been home, forever, and she knew they were losing space, or space was being taken away. Or at least what she heard in the cracks, in between.

This uneven land barely housed her family, and they'd taken from it. For the Olympics. For the sports. Rocky ground was where her legs first hit the land. Was where her bike first sled above the land, was where she fell face first into the floor. Rocky ground was where she kicked and fought on, dreamed and ran on. This was where she lived. It was bare, and it wasn't enough. And if they took here, what was left?

And she'd been participating here. She was apart of this: the crowd, the sport. And she didn't know. She didn't know, and her parents didn't tell her, and she didn't realize. And maybe after a while, she gave up wanting to understand, to seek out for herself.

The truth came as a stab, and Adesuwa was left bleeding.

.   .   .

We will expand. The building, seemingly never ending, pushed back a lot of things.

Once there were two countries, pushed back to a largely overpopulated village not too far from where she was standing. Her home ever decreasing till it was a dot, no longer a spot on the map.

.   .   .

Adesuwa felt bile push up her throat, the rush of adrenaline decreasing, overtaken by reckless and bitter thoughts.

Distractions don't last forever.

Her competitors—other nations—passed her by. She felt white-hot rage burning within her lungs, and she began to sweat, the crowd confused.

Adesuwa could do this—progress, progress, progress. She could do it and win, and succeed, in her own way, reclaim the land. A victory in being better. Her bike was just there.

But.

She breathed and breathed and breathed, then took many breaths, then fell to the floor. She spat and cried, tears fresh from her eyes. She felt the breeze as she was overtaken, and she felt the smallest in the world—a dot, to never expand.

She let her tears soften rocky ground.

.   .   .

Once there were two countries on Earth that jumped away. In the place they arrived, they became a clan.

Once they were vast.

Now they are called a minority group.

Generations.

FIRST THE RAPTURE, THEN THE PAPERWORK

Summer Jewel Keown

When the rapture came, Margaret was surprised. Sure, people had been talking about it for decades, centuries even, but she still wasn't ready. And what she really wasn't prepared for was all the paperwork.

Margaret had been clerking for the Heaven Admissions Office ever since she'd died in 1890. Having been born into a fairly well-to-do Maine society family, until then she'd never had to work a day in her life.

Passing through the office on her way in, she'd seen the little "help wanted" card in a tiny frame on the desk. Sure, she could have taken her admission and headed into the Pearly Gates, but she liked the idea of doing something useful for once. She'd asked the harried gentleman processing her in about it and seen his face light up.

"Thank God," he'd said. "Literally."

The day before the rapture, Margaret clocked in and poured a cup of coffee while she looked through her intake list. Glancing at the 800 names on it, she sighed. They would need to get more help again soon. With 55 million people dying every day and a good third of them coming through their doors, even divine help wasn't going to keep the waiting times down.

If only she'd known the deluge that was about to occur. Would it have been too much to have a little warning?

She'd heard that God could be a little mercurial, and that he was proud of his spontaneity. Sometimes his moods led to great things, like the creation of mankind or the invention of the iPhone, but it could also have its drawbacks, like the Great Flood or the Juan Pablo season of The Bachelor. So it was in line with his character that when he finally decided it was time for The Rapture that he would just do it and leave them to sort out the filing.

To be honest, God couldn't have cared less about getting everyone filed properly. That was Saint Peter's initiative. Margaret had never met the boss man in person, but she'd heard he could be a bit... detail oriented. She didn't mind. Margaret was born to run an office.

If only her family could see her now. Her father would have been shocked to not only see her working, but to see her in pants. Of course, that was normal these days, but back in her day it would have been the height of scandal to wear anything other than an ankle-length skirt. And her mother, well, her mother had said if she didn't act right that she would never find a good husband. Little did she know Margaret had certainly hoped that was the case.

·   ·   ·

When the rapture occurred, they all knew something was up. They were used to the sounds of the transport vehicles—the trains, ferry boats, and caravans. All the people chattering, excited, scared, anxious as they joined the queue. It all became a soothing white noise that Margaret quite enjoyed. But it had never been this loud before.

Margaret peered out the window and her mouth dropped open. The lines stretched off further than she could see, and she had perfect vision. Usually people joined the line one by one as they passed and made their way here. There was never an end to it, but other than major disasters like earthquakes and wars, it was unusual for the crowd to stretch off so far into the distance.

She ran into her supervisor's office to find out more. He was on the phone and held up one finger, signaling for her to wait. His forehead cratered with worry wrinkles; clearly something was up.

"I see…. I see," Mr. Chancy said to whoever was on the other end of the line. "We will do what we can." He hung up. He rubbed his eyes with his hands and looked up at Margaret.

"Well," he said, "It's time."

The entire staff stood at the front windows, peeking out.

"This is incredible," Margaret said to her favorite co-worker, Anita. "How are we ever going to get all these people through?"

"Well, technically we do have all the time in the world," Anita said, with a nervous laugh.

"Sure, but you know St. Peter's obsession with the wait time metrics," another coworker chimed in. Ben was a newbie, having only been there thirty years. He was always trying to prove himself to the boss.

Mr. Chancy came up behind them. "Well," he said, startling everyone. "I guess we all better get to work." They scattered to their offices and posts, and tried to pretend like this wasn't going to be the longest day ever, even longer than the days of the 1931 Chinese floods.

"Ready or not, here they come," someone called as the front doors were opened.

Margaret's first appointment went relatively smoothly, a minister who had been fully expecting the rapture for years. To be honest, she thought, he'd seemed a little too excited about the end of the world. But she filled out his paperwork in triplicate and filed it briskly, directing him to the door that led to the path that led to the pearly gates. I can do this, she thought. One person at a time.

That was fine, until the 64th person, when she hadn't had a break in hours. Each person had progressively more questions, all of which were reasonable, but which stretched out their appointments longer and longer. Even with the whole staff working furiously, the line outside only seemed to get longer.

Margaret took a moment to refresh her coffee, then pushed the button to tell the hostess that she was ready for the next one.

Her 65th appointment of the day rolled into the office, literally. A woman in her early twenties rode a bicycle in through the door and hopped off smoothly. Margaret was taken aback.

"You can't ride a bicycle in here," she said.

"Why not?" the woman answered. "I'm careful not to scuff the floor." Margaret took in her long blonde hair, dyed green at the ends, and all her tattoos, with some surprise. Things had changed so much since her day.

"You just… how did you even get a bicycle up here?" she asked.

"Oh, this bike is my baby. There was no way I was leaving home without her."

Margaret squinted at the bicycle now propped against her wooden desk. An aqua green single-speed with bright pink wrapped handlebars and slate grey fenders, it was clearly loved.

"Well that's something I've never seen in all my years up here, Ms… James." She couldn't help but laugh. It felt good to laugh after her day thus far. "Let's get your paperwork in order, and then you'll be free to ride in through the gates. I assume since you've brought it this far that they won't stop you now."

"You can call me Jenn. And I figure, with all those people outside, a bicycle is the least of anyone's worries."

"You're probably right about that," Margaret said. "We're up to our ears in new residents."

"You know," Jenn said, "It looks like you're a little swamped out there. I was a temp in so many offices back home. I could help you out for a little while."

"Oh, I don't know about that. There's a whole training to go through and…"

"We could give it a shot and see, and if I screw up you can boot me out and I'll ride off into the sunset. I only want to help."

Margaret hesitated for a moment, but she really could use the assistance.

"Well… all right. This is an unusual day, after all." She pushed the button to call in the next person.

·   ·   ·

They sped through admissions one after another, the stack of completed papers rising higher and higher. Forty people were processed through faster than she could usually have handled half of those. And Jenn was great with the people as well, warmly greeting an elderly grandmother, a college gymnast, and a circus juggler as though she hadn't only just arrived herself.

"This is amazing," Margaret laughed. "At this rate we'll be done before the next apocalypse."

"The next apocalypse?"

"Oh, yes. The rapture didn't take everyone, just the people who qualified. Which, obviously, there were a lot of."

"And then what," Jenn asked. "After you clear out this crowd, how do we celebrate?"

"You know, I have absolutely no idea."

"What do you mean you have no idea? Aren't you the Welcome Wagon?"

"Well," Margaret demurred. "I only know what we've been told. I've never actually been inside."

"You've never… But why? How? What do you mean?"

"When I got here, they needed help, so I took this job. Once you go through the gates, you don't come back. I don't know if that means you can't, or if you just don't want to."

"That's just wild. Surely you're curious."

"Well, yes, I am. But I like being useful. I figure that I'll go eventually."

"How long have you been doing this?"

"What year is it now?"

"2018."

"Oh wow. Time really gets away from you here. Let's just say when I came here, women still weren't able to vote. Doctor Who hadn't even filmed its first season. Not to mention bicycles had two very differently sized wheels."

"You know, I've always liked older women," Jenn said with a wink.

Margaret blushed and was, for a moment, speechless. She wasn't used to people flirting with her. They were usually still in shock.

"Sorry," Jenn said. "Too much?"

"Um, no," Margaret said, covering her mouth as she laughed. "Just the right amount of much."

•   •   •

They spent days upon days welcoming the newcomers, as far as days can be measured in heaven, typing up their records, and directing them to the Pearly Gates. The office became so full of papers stacked on every available surface that they could barely move. But instead of it being stressful and tiring, it was entirely pleasant.

Finally, they sent a woman through—a politician, if one could believe that—and pushed the button to bring in the next. But no one came.

"That's it!" someone called from the hall. Applause broke out from every office in the place. They'd done it!

Margaret turned and looked at Jenn. She was going to be sad to see her go.

"Thank you for your help. You have no idea how much it meant."

"I'm just happy to be of service," Jenn replied.

"I know I don't need to tell you that you just go through the doors and head down the path, then up to the gates, and that they'll open for you when you're just in front of them. I think you've heard the instructions a few thousand times."

"Thanks. I think I can remember that."

"I'm going to be sad to see you go," Margaret said, a tight feeling in her chest.

"You know," Jenn said. "You don't have to be."

"What do you mean?"

"What would you say to going with me? I'm sure there are plenty of places inside that could use a good office manager. Even heaven needs someone to run it."

"Oh!" Margaret said. "I always did think I'd go in when the time was right. But I just don't know!"

"Well, if you're not ready, that's ok. I just thought it would be nice to explore the place with someone friendly. No worries at all. Look me up when you get there?"

"Of course I will. I would like nothing better."

Jenn grinned and picked up her bike. She went to the door that would take her on her way to the gates. Turning the doorknob, she opened the door and paused at the threshold.

"Thanks for a wonderful welcome," she told Margaret. "I think I'm going to like it here."

Jenn walked her bike outside and climbed into the seat. She took a deep breath, and then began to bike away.

Margaret looked around the office. Seeing the stacks of papers, she felt a deep sense of satisfaction. They'd done well. But, she realized, the office also felt smaller, and it wasn't because the papers filled so much of the room. She glanced out the door, still hanging wide open, at the figure on a bicycle receding in the distance. It was like her heart was getting pulled out of her chest. And she knew.

"I've got to go, Mr. Chancy!" she called. "Thank you for everything!" She hoped he could hear her, but there wasn't time for a long goodbye.

Margaret ran out the door, barely pausing to shove it closed behind her. She began to run. Her legs burning, she realized that the last time she'd had any exercise was over a century ago. But still she pushed on.

"Wait!" she called, even though there was no possibility that Jenn could hear her, now a speck in the distance.

She tried to keep up, but the bicycle far outpaced her atrophied legs. Finally, she lost sight of it, and she collapsed, exhausted. Tears threatened to pour down her face. Now what? She knew that her time at the Admissions Office had come to a close. It was time for a new adventure.

So tired now, Margaret lay back and closed her eyes. She would get up in a minute, and begin her walk to the gates. She just needed a moment to rest her eyes.

A while later, she dreamed she heard bells in the distance. Or at least one bell. It seemed to be coming closer, until it was right there.

Her eyes popped open. The ringing didn't stop, but instead was right by her head. She looked up, and smiled.

Jenn stood there, astride her bicycle, ringing its bell.

"Well hey there," the cyclist said. "Strange place for a nap."

"You came back!"

"I decided I couldn't leave without you. If I need to put in a little office work until you're ready, I figure it's worth it. But I didn't expect to find you out here!"

"It wasn't the same without you," Margaret said, grinning. She climbed up to her feet, standing just taller than Jenn on her bike. Jenn smiled back.

"Well then," Jenn said. "What do you say we go explore together?"

Jenn helped Margaret climb onto her handlebars, and they rode through the Pearly Gates together.

THROUGH THE CEILING

Hella Grichi

S ix in the morning is such a good time to take a walk. It is a time when the air is still fresh, untainted by sand storms and car noises. It is a time where my mind is able to wander to beautiful musings, a time where looking up at the sky is actually an act of hope and not just to check if it finally got dark and the cursed day was over.

I look at the pastel pink sky and remember my mother and her bike of the same color. How she, in her oppression and silence, instilled in me the free spirit and independence I carry and cultivate today. How she, raised conservatively and passed on from male oppressor to male oppressor, managed to smile and pass on bravery and free will to me, her daughter. How thankful I am for the veiled rebel in the shadows, for my mother, for the fighter she was. A heroine in disguise. I remember how she juggled the kids, the housework, and her job. I remember how she went to work on her bicycle. -5 C°, black coffee and hearty smiles. That was my mother's day.

I was a latchkey child. The Germans call it "Schlüsselkind," keychild. My mother attached the house keys to a cord and I wore it like a necklace so when I came home at midday, I would always be able to open the door and never lose my keys. There was always lunch on the table. Always.

Lost in my thoughts, I clutch my jacket tighter; but the wind tugs at my short dress and I realize my tights aren't warm enough. I decide it would be wiser to go home and change into something warmer. I have to go to work soon anyway and still need to get some caffeine into my system in order to teach my little high school monsters properly.

On my way back, I notice a motorcycle approaching. "Nice legs, harlot!" the guy on the motorcycle shouts and disappears. I already got used to this daily senseless and cruel humiliation (which is in itself horrible given that the normalization of this horrendous behavior is in no way acceptable), but it is a pang every time. I don't want to give these types the satisfaction of a response, but I still feel so helpless. How a stranger can feel so entitled to your body will forever be a mystery to me. I know that wherever I would go, eyes would devour my whole body, undress me, tear at my heart, lick and scratch, trying to pull me down by mere eyesight. But resilient, gazing straightforward into the distance and into nobody's eyes, I went on.

By seven, I am sitting on my bed with a mug of cinnamon-flavored coffee. My eyes swiftly move to the raindrops pounding at the window like thoughts pounding at our brains when we overthink. It is a grey day. I miss my bicycle. I miss home. I miss my mother. The tires on her bicycle have been flat for a long time. I wonder if she could see me from wherever the dead go. Was she in heaven? Hell? In the Great Nothingness? Does she live in a cloud? Does she ride bikes in space now?

I feel an urge to curl up in my bed. That familiar urge that screams "Turn into a blanket sushi roll and ignore all responsibilities. Stay in bed all day and never get up again." It was a sad sight: to feel physically heavy, to feel as helpless as they had always said you'd be, to see the space portal in the ceiling go back to depressing whiteness just after you thought there might have been a gate of myriad colors and shapes to other dimensions. But now it is just a sterile, barren, and white ceiling. An asylum for the mentally defeated, that is my room, and I am the only patient. I am my own patient.

Reality tears me back to the painful here and now. It is time to go. I put on layers of wool and flannel to shield me from the harsh weather here in the Central West. There was no central heating, so when I leave my room, which is warm thanks to a little electric heater, it is like stepping outside, minus the wind. I stand in front of the mirror in the icy corridor, check my attire and fix the few rebellious strands of hair that escaped the bunch. I leave the house, lock the door, and go to school.

As usual, only a few students seem interested in my subject. The hours at work pass by meaninglessly. As a teacher, I should be feeling like an everyday hero, you say? But how many lives do we really touch every day? How many students look up to me and how many just want to have decent grades so as not to embarrass themselves in front of their tyrannical fathers that beat them hellishly for the least offense? I don't know and I am too tired to think about it more than I already did. So many of my students have so many problems. The least of their issues was the active and the passive voice, of that I am sure. A broken system raising broken individuals, if you can still call these Facebook-addicted monsters individuals.

Last week, I asked them about their favorite books. One still goes to the library, two told me about their favorite books with gleaming eyes. The rest broke out in useless chatter and superfluous laughter that showed me just how broken they truly are and how insignificantly small my attempts to involve them were. I smiled wearily and that was it. Back to the passive voice, babies.

The siren wails, signaling the end of the lesson. There is no soft school gong with a melody. It is literally a siren that sent everyone into a frenzy to leave the cursed classroom with the broken windows and the broken dreams.

Back to my warm room in the cold house in the cold town in this cold world. I have no escapes nor means of entertainment apart from the world I create for myself within my own four walls.

After lunch, I want to spend the rest of my three-hour break drawing, but I suddenly feel an energy surge in me triggered by seeing the clouds clearing up the sky. The pastel pink bike comes into my mind, calling me. I hesitate for a second but then I don't hold back: of course I would relish in those problem-free moments of cycling! Of course I would go feel the wind, the muscle pain, the speed, the excitement! I miss riding a bike so much!

I hop on my mother's bike that has no brakes—how ironic—and dash into the cold afternoon. "Highway to Hell" blaring through my earphones, I am feeling ecstatic again. I haven't felt this way in what seemed to me a long time. Somehow, I lost track of the stars and the ugly beauty of the universe that I became too fixated on my pain and the bittersweet longing for the past when all I had to do was take today into my own hands and thrust it far into space along with me and my dreams. Somehow, riding my bike into the never-ending road leading out of this stinking town, I feel like I am riding into space again, the way I used to before my spirit broke down like a dying steam machine. And unlike in my childhood, I realize what a powerful tool this bike was to make a point, even if I was proving it just to a few or merely myself. I laugh loudly and smile at the men passing by in their cars and motorcycles, glaring at me or looking at me with an expression of disbelief, curiosity or apathy.

So I ride a bike. So what? Why is this still so shocking? Look at me! Space, here I come!

Space isn't just for astronauts. It's the place you reach when you dare to rip the white monotonous ceiling of your room open and catapult yourself into Orion. It's the place you send yourself to when the floor begs you to break down and eat inhuman amounts of chocolate at 2 a.m. just to forget the trap you fell in. Space is the place where failures and successes interweave to form a web of hope and new beginnings. It is the place you whoosh to when they say you are nothing, when they say you are not enough, that you are tiny and helpless. Middle finger in the sky and dreams in space, that's how you do it. Go and show them what you are made of and that is stardust and cyanide.

Breathless, I return to my room. The same cold room in the same cold town, but my limbs and heart are so incredibly warm. I sink onto the floor happily and it is still as if the wind is whipping my hair back and forth. I am still feeling the pain of accelerating so ferociously. The sores on the palm of my hands and my dry throat are proof that I was alive not 5 minutes ago.

I go back to work for afternoon classes. I enter the classroom, smiling as always but this time a little brighter. Who knows how many smiles my little protégés get during their day? At least there would always be one from me, no matter how I truly felt inside.

This afternoon's lesson is about jobs. I ask them what their dream is.

"When I grow up, I want to be a teacher. Like you, Miss! You must be so happy now. I want to be like you and realize my dream."

It truly makes me smile. Maybe I am making a teensy tiny difference in the world. Their world. Maybe, despite my unhappiness, I could make the best out of the situation and contribute as much as possible. Maybe if I inspire even one child, I could call it a day. Maybe these myriad days of hopelessness would fly by if only I look at them in a different light, if I decide to be that very light. Maybe I could be someone's bike in space. Maybe I am here to rip the ceilings open and send them far, far into the galaxy.

ABOUT THE CONTRIBUTORS

Ayame Whitfield lives in Massachusetts and goes to school in New Jersey. She can be found on Twitter as @sumikocatherine and on Wordpress as avolitorial

Elly Bangs was raised in a new age cult, had six wisdom teeth, and once rode her bicycle alone from Seattle to the Panama Canal. Now she lives in Seattle, where she fixes machines, bakes pies, and writes a lot of upsetting dystopian novels. Learn more about her and read her work at elbangs.com

Elly Blue is proud to have founded the genre of feminist bicycle science fiction and urges you to submit your own stories to future volumes. She lives in Portland with her partner, cat, and dog.

Gretchin Lair is a pretend patient, AAA member, careful listener, and quiet advocate. She was once responsible for an accident while riding her bike and has felt bad about it ever since. You can contact her at gretchin@scarletstarstudios.com

Hella Grichi is a Tunisian activist, English major, and aspiring writer who is passionate about art, Celtic and Scandinavian folk music, fusion belly dance, and books. She is a co-founder of "Aspire to Inspire Tunisia," an initiative that organizes the only spoken word poetry events in English in Tunisia. She is on twitter at @hellagrichi and Facebook at @hella.grichi

Julia K. Patt has never met a used bookstore she didn't like. Her work has appeared or is forthcoming in *Escape Pod*, *Expanded Horizons*, and *Phantom Drift*. Follow her on twitter (@chidorme) for more.

Kat Lerner divides her toils between coaching, writing, and freelance fiction editing, her own work previously appearing in *Wings of Renewal: A Solarpunk Dragon Anthology*. In her spare time, she enjoys politics, potatoes, and arguing with her dog. @Kat_Lerner

Monique Cuillerier lives in Ottawa with her partner, children, and animals. She has always loved to write and will read anything, from history books to cereal boxes, but prefers Golden Age mysteries, hard SF, and literary fiction. She is on Twitter at @MoniqueAC and blogs sporadically at notwhereilive.ca

Osahon Ize-Iyamu writes speculative fiction and lives in Nigeria, where he is currently working on his first novel. You can find him on Twitter @osahon4545

Paul Abbamondi is a caffeine-dependent life form living in New Jersey. He likes puns, cats, drawing comics, and writing short stories. Please write to him at pdabbamondi@gmail.com because he also likes emails.

Summer Jewel Keown is an Indianapolis native transplanted to Ithaca, New York, where she works as an event planner. She spends her time running, riding bikes, knitting, and petting all the dogs and cats. You can read more of her work in the journal *HoosierLit*, or visit her at www.summerjewelkeown.com (up to and possibly after the rapture).

Tuere T.S. Ganges is a Jersey girl living, teaching, and writing in Baltimore, Maryland. A mother of 2 tall teenagers, her writing seems to have some sort of message for her kids...like how they should let go of the priceless family heirlooms if ever chased by zombies (great-great-grandma would understand.) Follow @tliereganges on Twitter.

SUBSCRIBE TO EVERYTHING WE PUBLISH!

Do you love what Microcosm publishes?

Do you want us to publish more great stuff?

Would you like to receive each new title as it's published?

Subscribe as a BFF to our new titles and we'll mail them all to you as they are released!

$10-30/mo, pay what you can afford. Include your t-shirt size and your birthday for a possible surprise!

microcosmpublishing.com/bff

31901064470471

...AND HELP US GROW YOUR SMALL WORLD!

More Feminist Bicycle Science Fiction: